IT'S HARD TO LOOK COOL WHEN
YOUR CAR'S FULL OF SHEEP

Roger Pond

IT'S HARD TO LOOK COOL

WHEN YOUR CAR'S FULL

OF SHEEP

Tales From

The Back Forty

ROGER POND

Pine Forest Publishing

Copyright © 1989, by Roger Pond

All Rights Reserved

First Printing, November 1988
Second Printing, September 1989
Third Printing, November 1989
Fourth Printing, June 1990
Fifth Printing, January 1991
Sixth Printing, August 1991
Seventh Printing, April 1992
Eighth Printing, August 1993
Ninth Printing, April 1995
Tenth Printing, October 1997
Eleventh Printing, June 2001

Library of Congress Catalog Card #88-92371

Publishers Cataloging-in-Publication Data

Pond, Roger, 1944-
IT'S HARD TO LOOK COOL WHEN YOUR CAR'S FULL OF SHEEP
1. Humor
I. Title

ISBN # 0-9617766-1-7

Published by Pine Forest Publishing
314 Pine Forest Road
Goldendale, Washington 98620

Printed in the United States of America

To Connie, Laura, and Russell
for their tolerance, affection, and the
occasional idea for a pretty good story.

Contents

PREFACE

It happens to everyone sooner or later. You are somewhere around middle age, and you realize you are too old to join the Jaycees but too young for a senior citizen discount. You still like to have fun, but often can't remember if you did.

Most people pass through this stage quickly and go on to lead normal, productive lives. But for others something snaps: They take up jogging, grow a beard, or quit their jobs to become free-lance writers.

At the tender age of 39 I already knew a beard is hard to keep clean (and my knees hurt when I jog); so I quit my job as a County Extension Agent and took up writing.

Like many others, I had "half a mind to write a book," and was afraid of losing the other half before the project was finished. I was comforted by the belief that half-a-mind is enough if you're willing to take twice as long.

Armed with these convictions, I have finally compiled a select group of my *BACK FORTY* columns into this volume. I hope you like it.

All material in this book is copyrighted by the author and has appeared in *THE BACK FORTY* news column, syndicated to newspapers across the country. These stories represent untold hours of sheep shearing, bull touring, and shuffling through that ubiquitous mixture of sawdust and manure found at county fairs.

I would like to thank all of those who have urged me to compile *THE BACK FORTY* into a book; and ask that they write with an address where any unsold books from this print run may be forwarded.

Thanks go also to Bonnie Beeks for long hours of editing to meet seemingly arbitrary deadlines, and for some creative title suggestions.

I am especially grateful to my wife, Connie, who spent days and months editing columns and designing the book, as well as assuring me it will soon be on the New York Times Best Seller list. (Bless her heart.)

Virgin Territory

Declining enrollments in agricultural colleges have furrowed the brows of deans and college administrators around the country. Some colleges have countered with recruitment drives to convince high school seniors that agriculture holds opportunity for them.

It was that way when I graduated from high school in the early '60's. The colleges were combing the countryside, looking for ag students. They must have been desperate, as I now look back on that particular time.

The colleges then were after the farm kids. They thought we probably already knew something about agriculture and might know how the boar ate the cabbage, as they used to say.

As it turns out, the colleges learned a lot from us farm boys. Nowadays they enroll a lot of city kids in agricultural colleges, and they're glad to get them, too.

It was about the time I was in college when someone originated the saying, "You can take the boy out of the country, but they'll likely send him back."

We could take for an example my old classmate, Howard Smeed, (not his real name). Howard was a farm boy from southeastern Ohio, down around Greasy Ridge as I recall.

His vocational agriculture teacher talked him into going to Ohio State University and enrolling in the College of Agriculture, but Howard didn't really want to go.

He had just finished a good senior year in high school and made better than $50 on his muskrat pelts, his coon dog had ten puppies, and his girlfriend had a job at the gas station. But the recruiters and his vo-ag teacher got to him, and he went.

He did take his muskrat traps, however. Howard had cased-out the Olentangy River during orientation week; and when the season opened, his four dozen traps were well placed. The river ran directly through the middle of campus, and Howard figured it to be virgin territory, as far as muskrat trapping was concerned.

He was right about that, and within a few days a number of pelts were hung to dry in his room on the ninth floor of Steeb Hall.

If it weren't for the murder investigation, Howard would have made tuition before Christmas. The investigation was traumatic for all residents of the dorm, but especially for Howard. The pool of blood in the showers and the little specks on the floor led directly to his room.

He was such a nice fellow — so quiet and polite; if he had cleaned up a little better he might have gotten away with it.

You can't blame Howard, really. He was under a lot of pressure. When you take a kid off the farm, put him on a college campus of 40,000 students, and give him a room on the ninth floor of a massive dormitory, where do you expect him to skin his muskrats?

Champagne Breakfast vs. Hair-of-the-Dog

It began as a friendly little race with my 12-year-old son, but I could see it was going to get nasty. The stakes were too high to be taken lightly.

We had a foot-and-a-half of snow at the time. The boy glided ahead on his cross-country skis. I followed on snowshoes.

I don't ski. When I looked at the kid's skis and saw they were made by Blue Cross, that was enough for me. I go with the snowshoes. They are light — fairly agile — quite practical really.

Suddenly a brain wave came over me. "I bet I can run in these things. I'll challenge that smart-aleck skier to a race," I thought. (Knowing full well you don't have to challenge a 12-year-old boy — you merely try to pass him.)

So I began to pick them up and put them down. The boy skied along ahead — swiish, swiish, swiish. And I was picking up speed — ker-whoomp, ker-whoomp, whoomp-whoomp-whoomp-whoomp.

If you've never seen a man run in snowshoes, it's hard to imagine the scene I'm describing. It reminds you of a gorilla sprinting through a hog lot: Lots of high-stepping, a sort of wild abandon, slightly out of control.

Then, suddenly, the kid heard me coming and looked back in surprise. There was panic on his face. He had the look of a boy being chased by a huge rabbit.

And I was gaining — Whoomp-Whoomp-Whoomp-Whoomp! It was the sound of a thousand rug beaters, bearing down on the confident kid.

The kid began to struggle. His poles were a'swinging and skis were kicking up snow. There was white stuff and nylon and wool socks going every which-way! But I was still gaining.

I began to feel like the old steam engine — Ker-whoomp, Ker-whoomp, whoomp-whoomp-whoomp-whoomp. There was no way to stop me now; it would take a derailment or someone throwing the switch.

It was then I realized this was no friendly race. It had become the old against the new. The old man in wool shirts versus the trendy, modern skier in his gaiters, nylon jacket, and Gore-Tex underwear.

I have waited for years to show these guys up. The joggers, the tennis players, cross-country skiers. All of them trendy in their fancy new clothes and expensive equipment.

The race took on a bigger meaning. Now it was quiche Lorraine vs. ham and eggs; bacon grease takes on safflower oil; it's the champagne breakfast vs. hair-of-the-dog.

It was then I knew America was rooting for me. We've been pushed around by these guys far too long.

But the kid is only 12, you say? So what! He started this thing--going out in the woods with all those fancy clothes and sleek new equipment. He was asking for it.

The kid looks back again, and I'm just behind him. The snowshoes are a'flyin'. I must have looked like a shipment of furnace grates with a heavy gale behind.

I pulled alongside, and the boy fell in a heap — laughing and rolling around like he was making snow-angels or something. He claimed he would have beaten me, if I hadn't made him laugh.

Who Gets the Manure?

It seems each industry has its by-product. For small-time sheep producers it's the wool. What are you going to do with six fleeces of wool after you have stuffed them into a giant burlap bag designed to hold five times that many?

But the industry says wool goes into wool bags, and there really isn't any alternative. I guess you would have the same problem trying to sell a basket of corn to the local elevator.

I've thought about stuffing wool into one of those burlap feed sacks and telling the buyer, "Yeah, this is a wool bag, but my wife ran it through the washer and it shrunk."

The question of what to do with the wool arose again this summer when the kids' 4-H club organized a shearing day for the lambs to be exhibited at the fair. One of the club leaders managed to hire a good shearer at a fair price, and we pretty much decided that the shearer's fee was a bargain for those who didn't want to shear their own.

Then we had to decide how to handle the wool. How much wool does a four-month-old lamb possess, and what is its value? Will the wool help pay the shearer's fee, or should it be considered inconsequential?

I was thinking if I had shorn these lambs myself there probably wouldn't be any wool, or it would be hard to distinguish from what was left of the lamb.

This reminded me of the situation facing a woman who got mad at her husband and bought a horse. She needed a place to board the critter, but was reluctant to admit she had purchased an animal she knew nothing about.

This woman went from farm to farm, shopping for a good place to board her horse and hoping to learn something about these animals in the process.

The first farm she visited charged $80 per month to board a horse. "Veterinary fees are extra, and we keep the manure," the stable owner told her. The woman thanked the owner and drove to the next horse farm.

When she arrived at the second farm she was told, "We charge $75 per month, vet fees are extra, our farrier changes shoes every four months, and we get the manure."

"Oh, I hope the farrier changes the horse's shoes, too," she said, but no one laughed.

So now the woman was beginning to learn something. She under-stood that horse ownership meant she could expect some vet bills, that horses need their shoes changed periodically, and the manure apparently has some value. She realized that manure is a by-product of the horse industry and can provide secondary income just as wool does for sheep producers.

Maybe a person could sell horse manure to mushroom growers, or get hooked up with a manure merchant or some type of road-apple shipper.

So when our horse owner arrived at the third stable she knew more about what to expect. The stable owner says, "It'll cost you $30 a month, you pay vet bills, and shoeing costs are extra."

She was so pleased with the low price for boarding, the new horse owner almost forgot about the manure. Then she remembered. "Oh, who gets the manure?" she asked.

The stable owner pushed his hat to one side and said, "Ma'am, for $30 a month, there ain't gonna be any manure."

Off the Wall

I still enjoy watching basketball — although it's really not much of a game anymore. Some folks marvel at those big college players and the pros who go flying through the air and slam the ball through the hoop, but that doesn't do anything for me.

We used to make shots like that everyday when I was a kid. We didn't call it the "Alley Oop" like they do now, but the play was the same.

In the old dairy barn there was a special signal for that play: one player would holler "off-the-wall" and another run up on the hay bales, grab a rafter and lean toward the hoop. He took the high pass and jumped for the basket, stuffing the ball through on the way down.

It was just one of the plays a guy had to make if he wanted to play in that league. Our barn had a big hay loft with a wood floor and baskets at both ends. Playing there was quite an honor — like Madison Square Garden — to the town kids whose moms would bring them out to the farm.

The off-the-wall play was good in the early part of the season when there was still a lot of forage on the court, but by January the hay near the basket had been fed, and nobody could climb up high enough to get the slam dunk. That's when the pure shooters came into their own.

In those days we had shooters! There were the two-handed set shots and several variations of the push shot. Our barn had cows below the court, and the ball would go down the ladder sometimes so all of us could shoot a wet ball, as well as a dry one.

Everyone had his own shot. It wasn't like today when they just jump up in the air and let fly. A kid's shot was dependent on what kind of barn his goal was in, as well as what else was in the barn.

You could pick the kids out at the high school games. The guy with the high-arching set-shot had a barn with a beam about six feet in front of the basket. He had to arch it over the beam.

The kid with the driving hook shot had learned to shoot around the corn-picker when going to his right. The one who took all of his shots from 19 feet practiced with a hay tedder on the floor and was limited to either layups or the long bomb.

Scouting reports on visiting teams covered what kinds of barns were common in that community, how much hay the boys baled (strong under the basket), and whether they milked a lot of cows (quick hands).

When you went to basketball games in those days, you could sense the talent assembled there. These boys had played in all kinds of conditions. They could shoot from anywhere; and,unfortunately, some of them did.

But the practice conditions were nothing compared to what we faced when we got into a gymnasium. There were bleachers down to the floor, and the in-bounds play was called "excuse me — two". You slapped the ball and hoped it didn't slap back. The referee gave you five seconds to get the ball in, but the crowd often permitted less than that.

Each gym was different. Some had a stage at one end and the home team would fill that with kids and other sorts of undesirables. Ceilings were low, but sometimes you could arch your shot a little at the end with the stage.

Size and brawn didn't mean so much in those days. We did it all with finesse. The big guys playing today would have brained them-selves on the light fixtures.

A Mind of its Own

ı It's always interesting to hear the old-timers tell about the days when farming was done with horses and mules. Most of those who farmed that way wouldn't want to do it again, but it's still fun to look back and remember the teams and the crews and the hard work.

Farmers were quick to recognize the value of the tractor when they had the opportunity to switch to more modern farming methods, but they knew the cold steel of a tractor could never quite replace the flesh-and-blood personality of the old work horse.

On the other hand, those of us born too late to remember the era of the horse will attest that the old tractors had some personality, too. That's why I will probably never own a really modern tractor: They just don't have a personality.

In my era, kids learned to drive on the old Ferguson, or Ford-Ferguson, as I think it was later called. This tractor had a mind of its own but was short of guts and totally deficient in brakes.

There were foot brakes on both sides of the little devil and a foot clutch on one side. If you had three feet you could push all three to stop the tractor, but most of us had to settle for jumping on the clutch with one foot and a brake with the other.

This would stop the tractor on the level, or on a hill if you didn't have a load on behind. But with a heavy wagon or implement behind, the 80-pound kid was like a flea on a trampoline as he tried to exert enough force on the brake to stop the tractor.

So you had some excitement ahead if you were heading downhill, or thrills behind if going uphill. In those days they tried to put most of the buildings on top of a hill so the kids wouldn't run into them with the Ferguson.

There was still plenty of room for error, though, and I have vivid memories of my most exhilarating experience on a Ford-Ferguson.

I had a summer job for the school district mowing grass at several school grounds, baseball fields, etc. The district had an old Ford with a rotary mower (bush-hog) on the back; and I was driving this from one school to another on a road past the state park, where some friends and I had spent the weekend camping.

It was necessary to stop at the camp to pick up some tennis shoes left there over the weekend; and I swung the Ford down the hill into the camp area, picked up the shoes, and started back up the hill in second gear.

Of course the Ford couldn't handle the hill in second, and if you've driven one you know the rest of the story. I pushed on the clutch to shift into first, and the tractor started coasting back-ward. I stood on the brake with the other foot, but the brakes on those things never did work. And you know the tractor won't go into any gear when it's moving.

The mower on the back was perfect for added momentum, and all I could see behind me at the bottom of the hill was the ladies out-house. You know how they put the little curved board fences around those things for privacy.

Well, me and my Ford just took all of the privacy out of that privy. Luckily there was no one in there. There wasn't even anyone around.

This was in Ohio, and you understand that's tornado country — and everybody has his own story about the twister that picked up the chicken coop and put it on the hay stack, without even break-ing the eggs. Strange things happen there sometimes.

I know if I was a park ranger, I'd rather report a tornado in the park than a Ford-Ferguson in the ladies outhouse.

The Old Hotel

Nearly everyone agrees that change is healthy for a community. We have to change in order to survive and prosper.

When times are tough it often helps to look at other communities that have dealt with tough times and somehow managed to survive. The little town where I grew up is a good example.

I grew up near St. Paris, Ohio; and like most small towns this one always had a hard time attracting and holding industry. Maybe it was just bad luck, but some residents thought the problem went deeper than that.

Much of St. Paris was leveled by fire in 1883, resulting in the loss of 13 homes and almost the entire business section. Estimates of the damage were in excess of $105,000. (I told you it wasn't a big town.)

One example of the town's bad luck was the carriage factory, which made St. Paris famous during the 1880's. Founded by a sign painter and his partner, this industry reached its zenith in the 1890's. The company exhibited their line of pony wagons at the World's Fair in Chicago in 1893 and soon began marketing these little surreys worldwide.

Then someone invented the automobile. Talk about bad luck! Just when we get our whole economy hitched up to ponies, Detroit cuts the traces.

The town learned an important lesson from the pony wagon business: A community's future is too important to get hooked up with the rear end of a horse.

For nearly a century, St. Paris boasted one of the biggest and most popular hotels in town. According to the *History of St. Paris*, by Kathleen Kite Brown, one Uncle Hiram Long moved into the Cline Hotel as a young man in the mid-1800's. He then proceeded to occupy the same room and sleep in the same bed for over 50 years.

The history doesn't say why the proprietor never got Hiram a new bed, but I suppose he had his reasons.

The hotel was quite a landmark and was still standing when I was a kid. I remember the signs on the door stating the building was condemned and would probably fall on you if you went in.

St. Paris was kind of a quiet town, but there was some excitement one night in the late 1800's when a fellow from Zanesville decided to commit suicide at the Cline Hotel. According to the town history, the man slit his throat and then jumped out the window of his hotel room.

This should be a lesson for those who are new to small towns and old hotels. The Cline was only two stories tall.

This poor man found his way back into the lobby, dressed in his night clothes and covered with blood. Two doctors were called in but couldn't save him.

In the final analysis no one could save the old hotel, either, and it's probably just as well. The town finally had the old building torn down in the 1960's, after it had been condemned both officially and unofficially.

After the hotel went down, some folks were real interested in building a motel to accomodate travelers and possibly attract some tourists. But each time the subject came up, someone would start talking about the old hotel and the man from Zanesville, and everyone would just lose interest.

Lost in the Remodeling

One of the great attractions of the old farm houses around the country is they are so conducive to remodeling. Building a new house is never as much fun as changing an old one.

People search far and wide for the perfect old home that is just right for tearing apart and putting back together again; and the older farm house is a sure candidate for a few changes.

There's really no way to avoid a remodeling. A friend once told his wife he would remodel the kitchen when the feeder calf price got up to $1.00 per pound.

Some will recall feeder calves have been worth $1.00 per pound only once in the history of the world, and it happened within a few months of his making that promise. A lot of people are hoping he'll do it again.

My wife recently decided to have the kitchen remodeled. The house is only a dozen years old, but we had it built with a very small kitchen. We were young at the time, and thought if we made the kitchen real small and ignored it, maybe it would go away. It didn't, and finally we had to make it bigger.

And really, no kitchen can be considered above remodeling. They're all going to get it sooner or later. Homeowners attack the kitchen for the same reason a dog goes after a skunk. Everybody knows better, but few can resist.

We had excellent carpenters though, so I don't have any room to complain. I used to do some little jobs like drywall work, but my wife couldn't get used to all the extra trim required to cover up my mistakes.

The kitchen is probably the worst place in the house to make changes. There are things in that room that weren't meant to be moved. It's easy to forget all of the things that go into a peanut butter sandwich, until you have to search for them, one-by-one.

The dishes all have to be moved, and the food has to come out and go into the kids' bedrooms. After ten years of trying to get the kid to clean his bedroom, it's embarrassing when we have to ask him for a can of soup.

Wives are especially enthusiastic about remodeling. I have always said if God is a woman the theories of evolution and creationism can both be accepted: she created the world in seven days and has been remodeling ever since.

This theory clears up a lot of scientific speculation. The dinosaurs may have withstood meteors, ice, and flood — but finally they were lost in the remodeling.

History makes more sense once you begin to see these events as a sequence of remodeling jobs. Entire civilizations have been lost in remodeling.

To me the excavations of Pompeii look less like a mountain eruption than the work of a sloppy brick-layer. The event is more believable when one realizes the whole thing could have started as a minor alteration in someone's kitchen.

The Romans and the Greeks had things pretty well in hand until they tried to update what they had built. They never could get it all cleaned up again.

Culture

No one has ever accused me of being cultured — at least not in the common use of the term. I feel more at home on a corn variety tour than at the opening of an art museum.

Last week I was able to attend both types of cultural events. One was a farm tour for learning about weeds and wheat diseases, and the second was an art showing and barbecue at the museum.

Both were quite enjoyable, and actually similar in many ways. The toughest challenge on a farm tour is keeping up with the group, and an art gathering is not too different.

I've always thought the farm tour travels in a cloud of dust and an art gathering also requires a certain amount of haze. The crowd for the farm tour was larger, but the museum group was more diverse.

Like most people, I find ways for overcoming diversity. When tossed into a diverse group, I seek out the farmers to talk with. Although I'm not a farmer, I feel more comfortable with them, and that keeps me from asking a doctor how the market is for gall bladders this year.

I think this makes my wife more comfortable, too. She figures I'm pretty much harmless if I don't circulate too much.

So I find out the price of wheat and how the cattle futures are doing, or try to learn how the fish are biting.

Like many families, my wife and I divide our cultural responsibilities. She takes care of the art, and I do the sheep shearing.

This is a common division of responsibilities but can lead to some tense moments at the museum. The wives enjoy the artistic events, but quiver with concern that the spouse will lapse into comments more appropriate for a horseshoeing.

The husbands are confident though, secure in the belief they probably know as much about sculpture as others in attendance know about hay balers. Most of us were on our best behavior last week, and I felt good about helping several friends learn more about art.

One fellow patron was having difficulty understanding a particular painting. "That's really a nice painting. I sure would like to see it when it's done," he said.

"I know how the guy feels," I said. "When I painted the kitchen, I ran out of yellow and had to panel most of one wall. I wonder if this artist has thought about paneling."

I wanted to explain the various schools of painting, such as the depressionist style, and use of long-handled brushes versus rollers and sprayers; but my wife was closing in on me and I chickened out.

Another friend was enthralled with a basket-weaving display. "I took underwater basket-weaving in college, but I could never stay under long enough to get one finished. I wonder how many baskets there are in the whole display?" he asked.

"Probably several cases," I explained. "Of course a case of baskets is not the same as a basket case. There may be a few of those around here today, too."

He wanted to know more, I'm sure; but his wife decided it was time for them to go home. Apparently it was getting about time for me to go, too.

Sacajawea's Revenge

I hate driving in the city. Something about city driving
gives me the feeling of being lost. Even when I'm not lost, I
know I will be soon — so I just start feeling that way the
minute I cross the city limits.

Part of my problem is that I don't want to be in the city
in the first place. Therefore, just being there is evidence that
I'm probably lost.

And have you ever tried to get directions in the city? I've
never been in a town of any size where anyone can give directions. They can take you there, but they can't tell you how to
do it on your own. A store clerk will ask, "Do you know
where Morgan & Floyd's is?"

I say,"No."

They say, "You know where you turn off Broadway to
go to the airport?"

I say, "No."

"Do you know where the Coliseum is?"

"No."

I always get better directions when I'm lost in the country
than I do in the city, but I've learned a few things about how

to ask for them. There's an art to giving directions and there are rules to heed when asking for them.

For example, I will no longer ask directions from a woman. It's just a waste of my time, a test of her patience, and no good can possibly come of it. A man can't take directions from a woman. The languages are different. I will say, "O.K., I turn to the left, and then I'm going south?"

And the woman turns toward the wall, starts waving an arm and says, "O.K., this is my left hand, right? So you just go by the school and turn this way, and you go by a store and out of town a ways and pretty soon you come to a road. Take the road this way," she says, leaning to the left.

"Then, I'll be going east?" I ask.

"How should I know?" she says. "We don't have moss on the trees around here!"

So, I don't ask them anymore. But it's just as bad for a woman to take directions from a man. They have developed a natural resistance to this sort of thing anyway, and the communications problem is just one more obstacle. When a man gives directions to a woman, he assumes she is going to get lost. The woman quickly senses this condescending attitude and just wants to stuff his map down his throat.

But he goes on drawing. "To get to the Johnson's you go out the drive here. There's a mail box on the right (he pencils in a box), and you make a right turn and travel about 1.86 miles and you will see a couple of grain bins on the left. (He draws some grain bins, with a weathervane rooster on one of them.)

So the woman is standing there thinking about Art 101, and the guy is drawing pictures of every barn and hay rake in the township — and finally she says, "That's O.K., I know where that stuff is." And she takes off down the road, turns this way twice and that way once and drives into Johnson's lane.

Some historians believe if it weren't for Sacajawea, Lewis and Clark would still be drawing maps.

A Fertility Problem

I enjoyed reading a recent article in which one economist was contradicting another economist on the causes and effects of current financial problems in U.S. agriculture. I didn't understand either of them, but it's always fun to see two economists enjoying themselves.

Besides, I have long held to the theory that all problems in the farm economy can be traced to the adoption of a single new technology, without fully understanding its long-term effects.

I'm talking about the Pill, of course. Everyone recognizes the new developments in farm machinery and chemicals, with their related effects upon farming practices. But few understand the subtle influence of birth control upon the farm economy.

Yet, the evidence is overwhelming. As we review changes in agriculture over the past thirty years, birth control runs like a common thread through each new practice and innovation, leading directly, I believe, to the greatly increased debt load of today's farmer.

For example, let's consider agriculture during the baby boom years; which, according to what we read, began about 1946 and accounts for all births between then and the present.

During those years a farmer didn't have a big $80,000 tractor or a $100,000 combine. When I was a boy, we had four little tractors that would hardly pull your boot off. (If you had a boot.)

But that's because we had four little boys to drive them. If we had one big tractor we would have one tractor driver and three fishermen. So Dad saved money with the four, little machines.

We would hook a mowing machine to one tractor, a rake on another, a baler a third, and pull wagons with the fourth. With this setup the family could bale 30 acres of hay in a couple of weeks. So we didn't need much land either.

And the kids were happy. Nobody had three-wheelers, or dirt bikes, and as long as we were baling hay we didn't have to worry about what the town kids were doing.

But then someone invented birth control, and you can see what this did to farming. Now we don't have the tractor drivers, so we have to buy a big machine that will cover 100 acres a day and a baler that throws bales in the wagon.

Then we needed more land to pay for the machines, and the kids never learned to walk because the three-wheelers kept their legs from growing. And the new tractors had cabs which took a lot of the fun out of driving them; so now the old man drives them himself.

With only a couple of kids around, the wives don't have to cook all day, and they need shoes and other expensive things so they can go into town. And they need a microwave oven to zap things with.

Just walk around a modern farm and you can see the evidence of a low birth rate. We do everything with machines.

I can remember when those big machines first began to appear on farms. The sociologists will tell you the first guys to buy them were innovators, but the rest of us just figured they had a fertility problem.

The Fruit Roll

Everyone knows teachers in this country are not paid what they are worth. Some are paid more than they're worth, and some are paid less.

We had the same problem when I was in school. In those days we tried to mitigate the low salary received by teachers with favors designed to help them cope. Many of our teachers were older ladies who were not married, so the neighbors or the school board or somebody would help them put up the storm windows, or give them a cord of firewood to help supplement their salary.

The old tradition of bringing the teacher an apple was founded on the same principle. Some say this also helped prevent scurvy in those areas where wild fruit was not normally plentiful.

But one of the most exciting, extra rewards for teachers at my school was the "fruit roll." The fruit roll was kind of like a surprise party; but instead of bringing presents everyone brought some fruit. Each kid would bring an orange or an apple or something for the teacher; and when the signal was given everyone would roll their fruit up the aisle toward the front of the room. Then the teacher would have all of this fruit to take home.

I admit this tradition may have been short-lived. I have never talked with anyone who remembers a fruit roll; and I can recall only one such event during all of my years in school. (There's a good chance that was the last one ever held.)

It was Mrs. Hardy's fourth grade (not her real name), and all of the kids had packed some extra fruit in their lunches. Most of us had no idea what a fruit roll was all about, but we figured the organizers knew what they were doing.

Just before the signal was given to roll the fruit I could see we had a problem. We'll call him Ed — and he was surely special. In those days we didn't have programs for kids who would benefit from special attention, but everyone knew Eddie needed extra consideration.

He had brought a banana for the fruit roll, and his seat was clear in the back of the room. You don't have to be a produce manager to know that bananas don't roll well.

The fruit roll was over as suddenly as it began. All at once there were apples, oranges, plums . . . you name it, rolling down the aisles and bouncing off the baseboards in the front of the room. Eddie threw his banana halfway up the aisle, and another kid tossed it the rest of the way. All in all there was a lot of bruise damage.

Mrs. Hardy became very emotional. I think she was trying to decide whether to thank the class or send the whole bunch to the office.

Count Your Blessings

Throwing things away has always been hard for me. I look at the price of new vehicles or modern equipment and say, "Hey, this old truck fits me just about right."

Everything has its limits, however; and just recently our old clothes dryer and washing machine both reached their limit during the same week. The dryer ground to a halt, and the washer just gurgled and groaned until we finally pulled the plug on it.

My wife had fixed that old dryer a thousand times. Each time the machine would break a belt or get a serious bind in its innards, she would fix it herself or call the repairman and he would bring it back to life.

The repairman liked working on our dryer, because he could always find some loose change or a few golf tees in the lint trap. The last time he fixed the dryer he said, "I think it will run for awhile, but if you don't buy a new dryer pretty soon, you'll have to start leaving more money in the lint trap."

Finally, the dryer quit and the washer missed the old tumbler so much, it just sort of folded up as well. I put both of them outside the back door to await a trip to the dump.

My wife was so embarrassed to have old appliances sitting outside the house, she kept telling our guests, "This place just looks awful with that washer and dryer down there under the deck."

I said, "Hey, don't point them out. Nobody knew those junkers were there until you told them."

I always thought having old appliances sitting around was a sign of affluence. It means you were finally able to replace something.

Then, too, I always look at old appliances and wonder if there isn't some way to use them. Bathtubs are famous as watering troughs, and a bathroom sink makes a pretty good feed box. What if we took the door off the dryer and stuffed hay in the front? Would the sheep eat out of it?

But embarrassment is a powerful emotion, and my son and I finally loaded the old machines into the trailer and took them to town.

This was pretty embarrassing, too; Russell was afraid someone would see him riding in the old International Scout we use to pull the trailer. Each time we met a car, I would say, "Get down! Get down! Someone is going to see you."

You can bet teenagers will be embarrassed no matter what you do. My sister and her husband own two Corvettes, and their daughter is humiliated when she has to ride in the station wagon.

But my son remembers all of those times we had to haul sheep in the back of the Scout, and the whole thing brings back unpleasant memories. If you have never driven into a fairgrounds with the kids in the front and the sheep in the back, you don't know just how much embarrassment can be packed into one small vehicle.

At times like these I try to make the kids realize there are others in the world who may be less fortunate than they are.

"If you think you're embarrassed," I tell them, "just think how the sheep feel. I'll bet they are mortified!"

Stallside Manner

I have always had great respect for veterinarians. They are such intelligent and good-natured people, a person just has to like them.

A large measure of this respect comes from the knowledge that these people got themselves through veterinary school; and even though I don't know for sure what they do in vet school, the thought of it makes my brain quiver.

I know a person has to be smart to graduate from a veterinary college. These students take the hardest courses in the university, and you won't find any dummies passing that curriculum. The vet students take things like organic chemistry, and physiology, and other courses I can't even pronounce — mostly just to show they are smarter than the rest of us.

A lot of college students will argue that you have to be awful dumb to take such difficult classes; but everyone will admit that once you are dumb enough to take 'em, you have to be pretty smart to pass them.

The confidence that people have in their veterinarian rivals the respect many folks reserve for their physician. And some farmers will readily tell you they have more faith in their vet.

I bring all of this up to explain why the vet has to be as careful with his diagnosis and his stall-side manner as the physician is with his.

The last time I was in the doctor's office I was reading an article in *Newsweek*, or some such magazine, in which a doctor was explaining the psychological side of diagnosing a patient's illness. The author said that while some patients want to hear that everything will be O.K., others want a lot of sympathy for all of the things that could be wrong with them. If you tell the second group everything will be O.K., they will be mad as hops.

The veterinarian faces a similar situation. The vet has to consider what the owner thinks is ailing the animal in question, as well as the owner's feelings about this critter.

A few weeks ago I asked a new vet student if the veterinary college teaches students techniques for gaining the confidence of the animal's owner.

The student said, "I don't know what they'll teach us in class, but I'll tell you about one of the vets I've worked for. A lady brought in her dog one day, and she talked to that dog as if it were her baby. 'Oh, my! Barfy hurt her little foot!' That kind of thing," he explained. "So the vet starts talking to the dog as if it were his baby. He talked to the dog all the time he was working, and the lady left as happy as could be.

"Then a guy comes in with a dog that was just a nuisance to him. The dumb dog was always getting hurt, and costing him money and so forth," he continues. "So the vet starts talking just like the owner. 'Let's get this mutt up on the table and see what he broke this time.' The vet treats the guy's stupid mutt and sends them both out the door — another happy client."

I laughed at the young man's story; then I wondered how I might look to the vet when I call him about my son's sheep? I'm sure he can tell I'm more afraid of the bill than anything else. Otherwise, I surely would have called him before things got to this stage.

The Silver Lining

You have to envy folks who can make the most of a bad situation. Some people have the natural ability to see each problem as a new opportunity.

This is the kind of person who can look disaster square in the eye and chuckle that it could have been a lot worse. I had the privilege of seeing such a talent in action a few weekends ago when the kids' 4-H club helped a farmer with a tree planting project.

We had an energetic bunch of kids, and although most of them were small, they were not afraid to work. The kids came prepared with shovels of all types and descriptions, giving rise to my biggest fear: that someone would break his dad's best shovel.

This concern was proven well-founded when one of the parents broke his own shovel just before lunch. I wasn't worried about the adults, though. I was more concerned with the kids.

My wife says I worry too much, but I've always felt a person should stick with the things he's good at. I adhere to the philosophy that even when you can't do anything, you can still worry about it.

On that particular day Clay's shovel became my first concern. His shovel had a crack down the handle big enough for a lizard to hide in, and I was sure this much-used spade wouldn't survive the day.

Each time the boy extracted a shovelful of soil, the old shovel would creak and groan like a barn door with a rusty hinge. But even though he worked like a badger, Clay's shovel didn't break.

I managed to put the whole thing out of my mind until late in the day, when I was working next to Clay and the landowner's adult son, Rich. We were busy digging holes and inserting trees, when I again heard the old shovel rasping and groaning.

I said, "Clay, I don't understand how you have been able to work with that shovel all day, and the handle still hasn't broken. It must be stronger than it looks."

The words were no more than out of my mouth when I knew what I had done. Anyone who knows anything about boys would have known better than to make a statement like that. I think he took it as a challenge.

The next time I looked up, Clay was perched atop his shovel like a raccoon on a corn stalk. Then he started waving back and forth as if impersonating a weather vane, and I knew the old shovel had met its match. Pretty soon the handle went creee-aack and the boy tumbled to the ground. "Drat," he said. "It finally broke."

I was thinking about the price of a new handle and hoping the shovel didn't belong to the boy's dad or his Grandpa. I wasn't sure what to say.

But Rich peered at the apparent disaster and saw the bright side. He looked at the shovel with its splintered, four-inch handle and said, "Well, Clay, now you have a good shovel for digging out the basement."

Going to Town

Living in the country has always meant a certain amount of isolation. You are a little further from the store than the folks who live in town, and the kids have to ride a bus to school.

This may seem like isolation to the modern generation, but some of the old-timers remember when going to town was an experience. You didn't just head to town everytime you needed a loaf of bread.

Of course the automobile changed all that. And with the advent of good roads, people started going to town anytime they felt like it. They didn't all go in the same way, however.

A friend's story about two old bachelors going to town on their tractor reminded me of the strange things we used to see on country roads. My friend says one of the two brothers would drive the tractor into town; but because he couldn't see more than 30 feet ahead, the other old guy rode on the back to give directions and point out obstacles.

I was reminded of the old man we used to see walking down our road toward town when I was a kid. Old Man

Johns must have followed Teddy Roosevelt up San Juan Hill, or at least the old fellow had a uniform from about that era.

He lived alone several miles from town and never drove a car. About once a month you would see him marching up the road in full uniform, looking like a captain in the cavalry who had somehow been separated from his horse.

We always figured he was going to town after groceries — and he would be seen walking back home that afternoon with a bag under his arm. But you could tell from his uniform and the tall leather boots that he wasn't just going for groceries.

He walked briskly, with each step of measured length and cadence. From his strident pace and the look of determination on his face, you'd think the old guy was drill sergeant for the toughest outfit in the Union Army. To us kids he was going for groceries; but I'm sure Old Man Johns thought he was marching through Georgia.

Then there was Frank Parker, who lived a few miles away. He never drove a car, either, but relied upon his horse to get him to town and back. Everyone knew Frank could have driven his Ford to town, but without the horse he never would have gotten home.

Frank's old horse was like a designated driver, only a lot more dependable. That horse never touched a drop of alcohol in his life and could find the barn in the worst of storms. After that, it was up to Frank to find the house.

The only real problem with the horse was that he couldn't jump sideways when he felt Frank's weight starting to slide; and then, not being a camel, the horse couldn't get down low enough for Frank to climb back aboard.

On these occasions a Good Samaritan would be called upon to extract the old fellow from a snow drift and give him a boost back aboard his steed.

It seems that most of the old guys are gone, or have moved into town. Sometimes when I see photos of the homeless in our cities, I say to myself, "Hey, there's Frank Parker! But where's his horse?"

Without that horse Frank would have been homeless, too. He was just lucky he didn't have to live in the city.

We Didn't Need Acid

Keeping in style has always been a problem for me. The only way I can keep up is to wear the same clothes for several years, and hope they are in style part of the time.

When I was a senior in high school my mother bought me a double-breasted suit so I would be in style for graduation. Those suits were so ugly they were out of fashion before I got off the stage with my diploma.

But the double-breasted keeps coming back, and when I graduated from college four years later the old suit was right on target again. I still have that suit somewhere, but I hope I never need it.

Just recently I was feeling sorry for folks who have to wear those faded jeans you see around town. Then my daughter told me those jeans are the latest in style. She says they are called "acid washed."

Clothing experts say acid washed denim is produced by washing the material with volcanic rock that may have been pickled in hydrochloric acid. This produces a bleached-out look, reduces the fabric's durability by 25 to 50%, and raises the price several dollars.

We had some pants like that when I was a kid, but ours got bleached from wrestling with tractor batteries or falling down in the barnyard. In those days a person wouldn't be caught dead in a pair of faded, white jeans like people are wearing now.

Our pants were called "overalls," and there was nothing tougher for daily wear. These pants were called overalls because they could be worn over anything. On a cold winter day, the average kid might be wearing three or four pairs of pants at any given time.

There were five boys in my family and Mother always ironed our overalls so they would look nice. This was quite a chore until she got her mangle.

Now, that was a piece of machinery! The mangle had a big, round drum which I think rotated against a concave to press the clothes. You sat in front of it, feeding the overalls into the machine, much as you would feed a wringer-washer.

The drum was operated with a foot pedal, and each time the concave was pressed against the clothes a big cloud of steam would belch toward the ceiling. Talk about power — using a mangle for wash day was like taking a road-roller to a cookie bake.

This machine would iron any kind of laundry, but my mother only used it for overalls. If you put a tan shirt though the automatic iron, the garment came out looking like a brown grocery bag.

Overalls rolled from this machine like paper from a typewriter. These pants were brittle. You had to bend them over a chair and jump on them a few times to loosen them enough so you could crawl in.

But styles change, and durability was a lot more important in those days than it is now. Acid washed jeans wouldn't have lasted two weeks at our house. Mother's automatic iron would have eaten them alive.

A Running Shot

While the fall hunting season is greeted with pleasant anticipation by many, it unfortunately brings confusion and bewilderment for others. The wives of hunters are often among those who don't totally understand why people go hunting — or what they are talking about when they get back.

This is sad, because so much can be gained by listening to one's husband. Most hunting stories only last a few weeks.

I have always thought hunting stories should be a family activity where even the children can participate by embellishing and polishing the original version. In order to make this a fun event for the entire family, I answer tons of mail each fall to explain hunting terms to non-hunters.

Here are a few examples.

Dear Mr. Pond:

My husband recently returned from a deer hunting trip on which he claims to have bagged a big four-point, with a running shot. He quit talking after I suggested he might shoot better standing still; and he never would explain to me what a four-point is.

Please send me some hunting terms so I can strike up a conversation again.

Signed,

Silent Partner

Dear Partner:

Your question is a good one. Few people understand what constitutes a four-point deer. This generally refers to the number of points on the antlers, but also depends upon what part of the country you are in. In the East, points on both sides of the antlers are counted, making a deer with two points on each antler a "four-point." In the West only one side is counted, so a four-point deer is one with four points on one antler.

It is becoming common practice for many hunters to use a combination of eastern and western count. Under this system the points are counted on both antlers (eastern count), and then the points are counted on one antler (western count). These two numbers are added together giving the "hunter count." This system makes any deer with antlers a three-point as a minimum, and skips into six-points rather quickly. Some hunters also count the ears, tail, and nose as points, but it's best not to mention this to your husband.

The "running shot" should be left alone, also. This is merely the common method of measuring in which a liquid is poured into a small glass and allowed to run down into a bigger glass.

Dear Mr. Pond:

My father and his buddies are always tossing about hunting terms, such as packing-in, still-hunting, and muzzle energy. Can you explain what these mean?

Signed,

Justin Case

Dear Justin:

The following is from my glossary of hunting terms.

Pack-in: 1) One method of getting your equipment into the house, 2) can also mean time to quit,as in, "Let's pack-it-in".

*Still-Hunting:*Usually refers to older hunters, who refuse to quit.

*Muzzle Energy:*1) Bullet energy measured at the rifle muzzle, 2) May also refer to an undesirable trait in hunting buddies: See "loose-jawed."

Good Equipment

This is the day to start my tractor. While this may not seem like a big thing to some folks, those who have seen my tractor will recognize the significance of the occasion.

This tractor has two starters: one that never did work, and a second that stands on the ground and turns a crank. Some would say that makes two cranks also, but we'll ignore these people as best we can. I think you get the picture — this is sort of a wind-up tractor.

I'm lucky my tractor work is confined to plowing the garden and grading the lane, neither of which takes much effort. If it took much effort, this tractor wouldn't do it.

I've always wondered why other people have tractors with electric starters, implements that fit the tractor, and tools that fit the bolts. They couldn't have come by it honestly. Certainly there's something suspicious about going to your tool box and finding it full of tools. What sort of terrible threats would cause family members to put the tools back in the box?

I realize it's not fair to hate people with good equipment, but a sincere dislike seems inevitable. They don't need that fancy machinery and probably just bought it to show-off. I've seen how they operate.

The good-equipment people are the ones who make livestock pens with Powder River panels and throw away baling wire instead of building things with it. Their pickup carries two bales of hay (unbroken), rather than four inches of manure and a pile of wire. They are the sort of people whose wives still fix breakfast. We shouldn't be critical, but you must admit, these folks do make quite a spectacle of themselves.

I suppose those of us with the pre-war machinery should be thankful we haven't been caught up in this wild and conspicuous materialism.

The old machinery does have its advantages. Let's remember there's a lot more steel in the old equipment than in this flimsy new stuff. Even after you subtract the losses from rust, the old machinery probably weighs more than the newer models. Someday this will surely pay off in the scrap iron market.

We should also remember that the depreciation has expired on the old machines, saving us a lot of tedious figuring and fretting over tax deductions. And we won't get stuck with a big bill for expensive parts — you can't get parts for anything that age.

Then, too, one of the major attractions of farming and gardening is the opportunity to work together with other family members, and this machinery certainly provides these opportunities.

"Hey, Russell! Tell your mother to come out here and help me start this tractor."

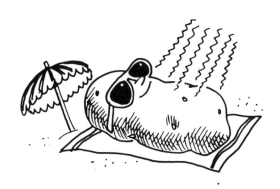

Potatoes and Other Tourists

I hate to keep griping about the tourists. Most of them are really nice people, and nearly all of us get caught being a tourist once in a while.

The state of Oregon has just bought a new study showing we are all tourists when we leave home. This ingenious study propels tourism past agriculture as Oregon's number two industry. Only forest products exceed tourism for expenditures according to the report.

This may not seem important to those of us who don't live in Oregon; but it is. It's important because it shows what a nice study can be purchased for a small amount of money.

Similar studies could help the rest of us in Washington or South Dakota, or wherever, prove that only a small amount of our food is produced on the farm. Most of it comes from grocery stores. And those who eat food are generally tourists.

O.K., I'll confess I haven't seen the study and for some people this might be a disadvantage — but not for me. My wife can tell you I don't need a lot of information before forming an opinion.

After wading through numbers that would choke a horse, as they used to say, I found the meat of the matter in the fourth column of the newspaper story where it stated that Multnomah County (that's Portland) accounts for 44% of Oregon's tourist income. I would have thought tourist dollars would be spent on the coast or at ski resorts.

I was also amazed to read that tourism is one of the top employment generators in Oregon with 53,000 jobs compared to agriculture's 32,000.

Then I found the statement that the study's economic data model only tracks U.S. residents traveling more than 100 miles from their homes. Now, we're getting warm.

In the last paragraph we find, "(the study) reports that travel generated $110 million in federal taxes on gasoline, airline tickets and personal and corporate income."

Now, do you suppose that everyone who travels more than 100 miles in Oregon is a tourist? And would you guess that when Howard Jackson flies from Portland to Wyoming to buy bulls, his airline ticket is a tourist expenditure?

How about on the trip back? What about the bulls?

For people unfamiliar with Oregon, residents of eastern Oregon sometimes travel 100 miles to get a drink of water. In that part of the country they have cows who can qualify as tourists. My wife drives 100 miles to Portland just to see if the stores are open.

Again, why am I telling you all of this? I just think it shows what an industry can do with a well planned study.

I am considering hiring myself out to do some economic studies for agriculture. I figure a potato is worth only a few cents at the farm gate; but if it can get to a restaurant 100 miles from home, it's worth better than $2.00 as a tourist potato.

A Good Shaking

My wife and I had a nice visit recently with some friends who operate a prune orchard. While a prune orchard may not sound exciting to a lot of folks, it is to me.

Our friends showed us the whole operation — from picking to drying. But the most exciting thing to me was the apparatus they use to harvest the fruit. This prune-picking machine slides up to a tree like a giant pair of pliers. Then, two rubber-covered jaws take a firm grip on the trunk and shake vigorously. The ripe fruit falls onto a rubber-coated table, which also fits around the tree; and the table delivers the goods into a small conveyer.

The prune picker reminded me of my third grade teacher more than anything else. Mrs. Lambert (not her real name) was not much of a fruit picker, but I can still see her sidling up to an errant third-grader, wrapping her big hands around him, and just literally shaking the prunes out of him.

My third grade teacher was from the old school when it came to getting a youngster's attention. When it comes to shaking things, a prune-picking machine is a lightweight compared to Mrs. Lambert. If a few trees had made her mad, I think she could have picked an entire orchard in a matter of minutes. I'm not saying we third-graders didn't deserve a little shaking now and then, but I'm happy to see that styles of teaching have changed.

We had a lot of school truancy when I was a kid. Some youngsters stayed home to help on the farm, but others just needed time to recuperate from whiplash.

In those days, the third grade was where a person learned to write legibly. Mrs. Lambert wasn't much interested in new writing styles. If no one could read your writing, it was pretty hard to sell it as creative.

Some of the kids learned this quite easily, but for others it was difficult. We pressed down too hard, or squiggled too much, and our *D*'s looked like *O*'s.

Nothing made Mrs. Lambert more violent than bad writing. She would swoop down upon a sloppy writer like an owl catches a mouse. Then, she would take the offender's hand and try to help him.

If you have ever tried to write with a young python wrapped around your arm, you have some idea of how this technique is applied. To this day, anything I write in longhand looks like someone has hold of my writing hand and is squeezing the blood out of it.

I will always remember the afternoon I was writing the word *hay*, when Mrs. Lambert grasped my hand and tried to smooth out the letters. We got past the *H* and the *A* and I was just finishing the *Y*, when she hollered, "You're pressing too hard!"

With that she shoved the pencil across my yellow pad, creating a trench several pages deep and ending with a black hole about the size of a BB. The pencil lead was shattered.

"See, I told you you're pressing too hard. Now, look what you've done!" she said.

The Bummer

I could tell she didn't understand. How could she, at her age?

She could probably see the anguish on my face and the bags under my eyes. She could hear the tone of quiet discouragement in my voice. But she couldn't really understand.

"What do I need to put this together?" I asked. "Is the tube and the nipple all there is to it?"

"You have lambs to feed?" she asked. "How many do you have?"

"Just one," I said.

"Oh. You don't want that. It's much easier to just feed them on the bottle. With this you need a bucket, and you have to wash it out after every feeding. For one, I'd feed it on the bottle. That's what I do."

"Could you tell me what I need to put this together?" I asked, my voice cracking slightly.

"Well, no. I've never used one of those," she said. "I just feed them on the bottle."

It was all I could do to hold myself together. I wanted to blurt out, "What do you think I'm doing now? Don't you understand what it's like to have a bummer lamb running up onto the porch at night and baahing at the front door?"

Or to know that there is this little animal hiding out there in the darkness, just waiting for you to try to leave the house?

I could have given her the fatherly lecture: "Now see here young lady. In the first place, you don't have to tell me how to feed orphan lambs. I know all about the little bummers!

"I'll also have you know, this isn't my lamb. It belongs to a sheep! A female sheep! And I won't stand for any female telling me what to do with it!"

I can see now I was getting pretty riled.

All I wanted was one of those little lamb-bar nipples and a tube, so I could rig up a cold-milk feeding system like they tell about in the books. I just wanted to get this lamb on a self-feeder so I could stop running around all day with a lamb chewing on my pants leg.

Even at her age, the feed store clerk should have known what happens when a ewe won't claim one of her lambs, and you suddenly become nursemaid to the rejected and downtrodden.

Doesn't she know what it's like to lie awake worrying that the poor little thing might die? And later, to come face to face with the possibility that it might not?

Besides, it's not my lamb. It belongs to a sheep. And the sheep belongs to my son.

But he's busy — with baseball practice and golf and all sorts of things. If I left it to him, it would die for sure.

So, we're gonna give this critter another chance. We'll just put one end of this tube in the nipple, the other end in this container of cold milk; and we're going to make a sheep out of this lamb if it's the last thing the little beast ever does.

Door-to-Door Salesmen

One of the privileges of living in rural areas is the occasional visit from door-to-door salesmen. You never know when one will drop by. They are such creative fellows that each visit is a new experience.

We used to get a lot of visits from particular religious groups also, but my wife put a stop to that. She simply cannot be rude to anyone and always lets the callers go through their entire spiel. However, her interest in religion prompts her to argue various points of theology in an attempt to convince the caller his or her theories are ill-founded.

These folks quit coming. They figured there was no use in sending out the faithful only to have them return as Methodists.

I tend to sympathize with representatives of church groups, but my style with door-to-door salesmen can be described as politely abusive. A visit a few years ago from book salesmen serves to illustrate.

It was about 3:00 P.M. when my young son and I answered the door. The two salesmen seemed surprised to find a man home in the afternoon. One of them asked if Mrs.

Pond was home and offered to return later when I told him she wasn't.

"Oh, no, that's O.K. You can talk to me," I said.

"Well, we have the new learning guides that everyone is getting for their elementary school students. Usually the fathers ask us to talk to the Mrs. about it," he explained.

"I think I can handle it," I stated. "Tell me about it."

The salesman looked at his partner with obvious apprehension, and then began his pitch. He knew our children's names, what grades they were in, and all of our neighbors to the south. (These boys had asked a lot of questions someplace.)

"I'm from Georgia. I'll bet you could tell by my accent. Have you ever been to Georgia?" he asked in his best drawl.

"Nope."

"Well, have you ever been in the East?" he probed.

"We're from Ohio," I allowed.

"Oh, great! I was born in Erie, Pennsylvania. Isn't that something!"

"That's nice," I said.

He looked at his partner again. The partner had moved closer to the door.

"We have these learning guides that everyone is getting for their kids. They are really helpful for reports and learning how to do math problems and everything. I suppose you probably have encyclopedias and all. Where do your kids get information for their reports?"

"At the library," I said.

"Well, these are nice learning guides. There are two of them. One is all on science and biology; and the other is math in the front, and the back half is a Bible."

That seemed a strange arrangement to me, but I held my tongue.

"Your neighbor, Craig Wolfe, liked the way the math book explains the problem, and then gives the answer. What do you like most about these learning guides?" he pleaded.

"I think we'll continue to get our information at the library," I finished him off.

With that the salesman folded his books, smiled nervously at his partner, and both jumped for the door.

As they drove down the driveway, I turned to my son and said, "Let that be a lesson to you, Russ. Get yourself an education, so you won't have to sell books door-to-door."

About 30 Seconds

If you read question and answer columns in the daily papers, you can understand the problems associated with accumulating questions and then trying to come up with answers for them. While questions can be kept indefinitely, answers don't store well and must be dispensed promptly, or even hastily, before further deterioration can occur.

I shudder to think of the perfectly good answers I have thrown away, simply because there was apparently no question to go with them. However, I have matched up a few and wish to share them with you.

Dear Mr. Pond:

We recently bought a farm with two acres of pasture and have stocked it with six goats, four sheep, two cows, a horse, and eight chickens. These species seem quite compatible, and the animals are all having a good time; but the pasture has stopped growing grass.

My husband reads a lot and is in to modern concepts of sustainable agriculture, species compatibility, and stuff like that. The county agent says we have too many animals, but my husband thinks it's a problem in species balance. What do you think?

Signed,

Knee-Deep in Vermont

Dear Knee-Deep:

I agree with your husband. Proper pasture management is always more dependent upon species balance than total numbers of animals. You might try attacking the problem by obtaining a couple of wolves or possibly a small lion. Either of these species should put things back into balance. I would recommend the lion, as you could use its manure to keep the goats out of the garden. (See next question.)

Dear Mr. Pond:

I've been told that human hair repels deer and is effective in keeping them away from fruit trees and gardens. My uncle is a barber and has offered to let me sweep his shop for the hair. Do you know anything about this?

Signed,

Deer Lady

Dear Deer Lady:

I haven't heard about your uncle's offer, but I have seen deer frightened by human hair. Red hair seems to scare them most severely. However, deer don't pay much attention to hair unless someone is wearing it.

The most effective application of this technique is to run into the garden, pulling hair out in small handfuls, and throwing it at the deer. Associated screaming and hollering also helps.

P.S. It would be nice of you to sweep your uncle's shop.

Dear Mr. Pond:

We are new to country life and are trying to learn the terminology tossed around by our farmer neighbors. Bulls, heifers, wethers, mountain oysters; it's all Greek to me.

Can you tell me what's the difference between a bull and a steer?

Signed,
The Greek

Dear Greek:

About 30 seconds.

Keep those questions coming.

Heredity

I have almost given up on dietary studies. Ever since the USDA recommendations during the Carter administration came out strongly for peanuts, I have been suspicious of studies.

Now I read that two new studies in Finland and the United States show coffee drinking is not bad for your heart. A 1985 Johns Hopkins University study showed just the opposite. About the time we get everyone off the coffee and taking cold showers instead, we get a new study saying coffee drinking isn't related to heart disease.

The new research found that many of the coffee drinkers in the Johns Hopkins study were also smokers. Now they figure the coffee cup in one hand was not as important as the cigarette in the other.

This revelation comes on the heels of another study showing that creases in the earlobes is probably not related to heart disease, as was previously reported. An earlier project found that people with creases in their earlobes were much more likely to suffer from heart disease than those without such creases.

The earlobe theory was brought into question when someone noticed that creases in the earlobes increase with age. The theory is that older folks may have more heart problems, so it might not have been the earlobe creases after all.

This shows how much detail goes into some of these scientific breakthroughs. What passes for research nowadays is sometimes just a survey showing that people who drive tractors are more likely to buy seed corn than those who drive taxis.

There was a time when doing a study of earlobes would get a person a big laugh, or a fat lip at best. But now, you can get a nice chunk of money for doing this type of work.

There are a number of studies I would like to put together if I had the time. Most of them wouldn't take much actual work, but you'd be surprised just how little it takes to keep me busy.

For example, I'm pretty sure a well-planned study would show that orange tractors are harder to start than any other color. No one has ever studied this phenomenon to see what's causing it, but my old Allis Chalmers will almost never start without a lot of cranking and thumping. (I do the cranking and my heart does the thumping.) If someone wanted to prove that orange tractors are bad for your heart, this would be a natural.

My father had an old Allis Chalmers when I was a kid; and it's no small coincidence that tractor was orange, too. My brothers and I used to drive the old Allis until it ran out of gas, and then spend the rest of the day trying to get it started again.

I am almost sure someone could put together a study to show that orange paint makes these tractors hard to start; and if this research were carried one step further, it would show the problem is hereditary.

Not only are these tractors slow starters, but the man who owns an orange tractor will likely admit that his father also owned one. Now, if that isn't heredity, I don't know what is.

Le Farm Brut

The recent death of a famous French artist reminded me the road to fame and riches is not only poorly marked, but strewn with potholes and roadapples. Few can travel it gracefully.

The artist was Jean Dubuffet, who passed away at the age of 83, after having a tremendous impact upon art since World War II. He is survived by his wife, Emilie.

As far as I can tell, being survived by his wife is about the only traditional thing Jean ever did. But he became famous for breaking with the traditions of his day and setting his own course in art as well as life.

We could ask, why did Dubuffet succeed where many have tried, but failed, to slice the Dijon as they say? What enabled him to withstand criticism and ridicule, and to become famously controversial while others became infamously obscure.

I think Dubuffet went for it, whereas most of us only make a stab at it, and then back off. If you want to be controversial you have to go all the way.

For example, Mr. Dubuffet said in his published writings all that mattered to him was energy, spontaneity, truth to self, and with these qualities, a spirit of insubordination and impertinence.

I should point out that others have tried this creed but succumbed to various human frailties. Some starved and others were beaten to death with a cue stick.

When I was a kid I could be pretty controversial, but I never quite got it all down. The spontaneity and insubordination stuff was easy, but there's a knack to being controversial, rather than just a pain in the neck.

Only a few can make the jump from "kind of strange" to "truly controversial". You've got to act crazy enough so people stand back and watch, instead of trying to beat some sense into you.

If a farmer wants his obituary to read, "Howard Swartz, the controversial farmer, passed away Sunday at the age of 97," he needs to take a new approach. He needs to take advantage of the controversy around him.

When the corn rows look like someone planted them in his sleep, we shouldn't accept flack from the neighbors. We should say, "Those rows may look crooked to the traditionalist, but I see them as spontaneous and impertinent, possibly with just a tinge of insubordination."

If the corral fence is falling down and no one has the time or lumber to fix it, we can comment about that picturesque old fence doing its best to contain those picturesque old cows (that are too poor to keep and too cheap to sell).

Dubuffet coined the term, *L'art brut* or "art in the raw," to describe the style he advocated. When things aren't going well we could all use some non-traditional terminology to help us out.

How about, *Le farm brut*? "Farming in the raw" could explain a lot of things.

How to Order a Steak

The class will please come to order. Today we will discuss the proper way to order a steak.

I understand that some of you boys are from the farm and you may have acquired a few habits that are not considered proper in the fancier types of restaurants. I will do my best to explain why these habits are objectionable, and try to help you understand proper terminology.

First, we should consider the universal terms for describing how you would like your steak cooked. These are: rare, medium-rare, medium, medium-well, and well-done. You can remember these simply as degrees of raw and burned, with "rare" being raw and "well-done" meaning burned.

Now, I understand that local terminology is popular with some of you fellows, but I want you to be able to order a steak anywhere without embarrassment. Orders like, "Chase it through the fire", or, "burn everything but the rope" will get you into trouble sooner or later.

We should also clear up the fallacy that you can tell how much money a man has in his pocket by the way he orders his steak. This story says that the man with the most money in his pocket will order his steak rare.

This is not true. The man who owns cattle will almost never order his steak rare even though he may have quite a bit of money in his pocket. In fact, he may often have all of his money in his pocket, but still won't order a rare steak.

This is because the cattleman feels sorry for the rare piece of beef. He looks at it sadly and says, "If we could have just caught this one a little sooner, I think he would still be alive." Or he may say, "Ma'am, if you would bring me a doggie bag, I think I'll take mine home and feed him another thirty days."

On the other hand certain types of businessmen, especially bankers, like their beef rare. Bankers are a notably bloodthirsty group. This doesn't mean they have a lot of money but is more likely a result of their dislike for cattle.

So we can forget about the money-in-the-pocket theory of steak cookery, and just remember the cattleman likes his beef well-done. That way he knows it's dead, and he doesn't have to worry about any vet bills or future expense as a result of buying the thing.

What should you do when you are served a piece of beef that is not done to your liking? Well, if it's overdone you might as well eat it, because more cooking won't help any.

But if it's too raw, you should first look around the table and see who's there. If the other guests are farmers, you can use the comments mentioned earlier.

If there is a veterinarian present you might say, "I swear, Doc, this animal was just fine a few minutes ago, but he sure looks sick now, don't he?" Or, "If I use the steak sauce he probably won't heal up as well, will he?"

About this time your wife will suggest you send the meat back for further cooking, or cease with the corny comments.

That's one of the problems with wives. But that's another subject. Class dismissed.

Get Yourself an Education

It all looked so easy. One fellow backed the trailer into the water and his buddy deftly manuevered the boat into position. Then with a roar of the motor and the thrust of 60 horses the boat glided onto the trailer.

I was too busy trying to keep my balance while standing on the tongue of my own trailer to see the entire operation. Maybe I didn't really want to watch, anyway.

My boat was floating off to one side, and the winch rope was wrapping itself around my leg. "Climb over the bow and push the boat back toward the dock," I shouted to my son.

The boy was too busy watching the Bass Tracker® to fully understand my instructions. It's hard for a kid to see the advantages of a boat with a manual-start motor and an anchor made from a paint can, when you have these flashy bass boats roaring up and down the river.

But no one said economics is an easy subject, so I tried to explain it the best I could. "I'll bet they didn't catch any more fish than we did," I surmised.

"Bet they did," he grumbled.

"Our fish cost less," I countered.

"Did you see how they just drive those boats up on the trailer?" the boy asked. "I sure would like to have a boat like that."

"Well, you could have one if you didn't ride bicycles, or eat, or wear clothes; but you still wouldn't be able to make the payments," I explained.

Then I described the hazards of sitting in a boat with seats three feet in the air, where a guy's wife would have an easy shot at him if someone told her how many dining room sets are invested in a craft like that. And I explained the need for duck decoys and shotguns and other little necessities that some people may not have in their budget.

I emphasized the importance of living in moderation and not getting carried away with material things. My lecture skimmed the basics of personal finance and skirted the edges of philosophy and religion.

I described the need for a good education, so that a person won't have to work in a factory for the rest of his life — the feeling of accomplishment that comes from earning a college degree, or operating your own farm or other business.

I recalled my parents' philosophy: "Get yourself an education. That's one thing they can't take away from you."

I imagined that bass boats are one of the things they can take away from you; and the importance of a young man saving his money for college became even more obvious to me. One of those boats is the equivalent of two years on full scholarship.

All of this went through my mind as I watched the fellows with fancy boats and new four-wheel drive trucks load their equipment and head up the road.

As I sat there in the parking lot, my entire life passed before my eyes. Like many other graduates of the sixties, I wondered if we had done the right thing. We all know they can't take a person's education away; but you can't eat it, and you surely can't fish out of it.

Breaking to Lead

Never in the history of Tuesday night wrestling have we had such an exciting match as this one. In one corner we have two puny 4-H members who will attempt to corral, wrestle to the ground, and otherwise humiliate four big, fat lambs which have been known to jump over tall fences and small buildings in previous events.

Never before have we seen two kids take on such a group of savage beasts with only their bare hands, a rope halter, and occasionally their feet to protect themselves. It won't be a pretty sight, but the showdown had to come sooner or later.

For months these two teams have shouted insults at each other and now it's time to decide who's taking whom to the fair. It could have been settled peaceably if the fences were better and the vacations shorter, but now the whole thing has gotten out of hand.

Some youngsters avoid the big fight by working with their animals for months ahead of fair time, and their critters may arrive at the fair as tame and docile as can be. But then there are those cases when things didn't go right, other activities got in the way, and the best of intentions just didn't work out.

The road to the county fair is paved with good intentions (as well as roadapples, sheep pellets, and meadow muffins). Things just never go quite the way they are supposed to.

Sooner or later there comes the day when Junior asks, "Dad, do sheep sleep on their backs?" Or daughter says, "I don't think my steer likes me. When I jump into the pen, he jumps out."

Everyone has his own system for getting animals ready for the fair. Most concentrate on the physical condition of the animal, making sure the pig is muscular, the steer isn't too fat, and the lamb is clean around the armpits.

My kids recognize that mental conditioning of show animals can be as important as physical exercise. They understand the panic a dumb animal must feel when faced with large crowds and unfamiliar surroundings. And they assure me no one has dumber animals than theirs.

So they teach the lambs how to handle terror without suffering emotionally. Our critters are always able to run, jump, and tear things apart without feeling the least bit guilty or embarrassed.

The mental conditioning goes right along with physical training. Once a good panic is underway, all of the animals get plenty of exercise jumping over gates, running through the corn, and tearing down the clothesline.

If anyone asks my kids whether they've exercised the animals, they can truthfully answer, "Oh, yes. Oh, yes."

One can always tell which animals have been mentally prepared for the fair. They don't stand around and look dumb when they come off the truck. These beasts take two jumps past the scales, drag the owner through the barn, and head straight for the corndog stand. They know how to have fun.

I know a lot of people feel bad when these nice show animals are sold for slaughter. I too used to feel sorry for the animals; but that was before I got to know them better.

Fruits and Nuts

The mental health counselors will tell us people are faced with increased levels of stress at particular times of the year. In logging communities it's the winter inactivity that brings on increased mental strain. In farm communities it may be harvest time or planting time that pushes people to the brink.

Where I live huckleberry season seems to be the peak for emotional disturbances. There's something about dropping those tiny berries in that little bucket that causes people to lose their bearings.

A psychiatrist friend tipped me off to the situation several years ago, and I now stay out of the woods during the late summer. My friend says he saw the same type of mental disturbance with mushroom hunters when he practiced in the East.

"You wouldn't believe what some people will do for a few huckleberries," my friend says. "Once they get a taste, there's not much you can do but keep them away from the rest of society. Once the blue color disappears from their fingers and the stammering stops, you can talk to them, but they're not quite normal.

"It's hard to understand how those little fruits can cause so many people to go nuts," my friend continues. "Nothing is more pitiful than a grown man sitting in the trail, crying because he spilled his can of berries."

"That is a sad sight," I admitted. "I think it's that little 'poink, poink, poink' of berries hitting the bottom of an empty bucket. It's like water dripping on your head."

My friend says the incidence of child threatening and wife badgering is quite high among huckleberry pickers. The kids report being held captive in the woods and forced to pick berries until their can is full, or until the family has reached some arbitrary and unreasonable quota of fruit.

Wives of huckleberry pickers face a double jeopardy. Besides having to pick fruit like everyone else, they also are subject to guilt feelings that come with a freezer full of berries and no pie on the table.

I have seen huckleberries do terrible things to people, and would admit to threatening the kids myself, when they pester me to go home or fail to meet their quota. I say things like, "No pick — No pie." Or if they pester too much, I suggest, "Why don't you go play with the bears?"

My psychologist friend tells about the guy from Chicago who showed up in the mountains looking for berries. "There we were, standing on a logging road when this guy drives up in a big, black Lincoln and says he wants to buy some berries. He has been lost since 8:00 A.M. and offers me $200 for a quart of huckleberries," the friend says.

"Isn't that crazy?" he continues. "The guy must have been a complete nut!"

"That is something," I said. "What did you do with the $200?"

"What do you mean? I didn't do anything with it," my friend says. "I only had a couple of gallons and it was almost dark. There's no way I could sell him any. But it just shows how crazy some of those people can be about a few berries."

Oats, Peas, Beans, and Baseballs Grow

There it was, about halfway down the bean row. Just like a long lost friend — my baseball. I don't know how it got here, but here it is.

Wait a minute; this isn't mine. My ball went into the wheat field thirty years ago — and 2,500 miles away. But I've never stopped looking for it.

It was the best hit I had all day. A sharp rap off the catawba tree and over the fence. "Into the sun deck", as they used to say.

A hit like that is truly an emotional experience. You feel good about the mighty blast but dread the impending search for the baseball.

And we did hunt them. When a ball left the playing field both teams filed stoically into the neighboring crop and lined up for the search.

If the field is in corn, the ball is easily found. All one has to do is walk the rows. But when it's wheat or alfalfa, things get tough.

In wheat or alfalfa we would walk three or four abreast and search the ground, hoping to see the ball, or possibly step on it. When that failed, we'd lie down and roll until someone detected a lump under the foliage.

I've sometimes wondered how much crop damage is incurred as a result of lost baseballs, but Dad never seemed to worry. He was often the guy who hit the ball; so I guess he couldn't say much.

In those days a lost baseball was the equivalent of a players' strike. Nothing moved until the ball was found.

Kids got new baseballs for Christmas or picked up the occasional foul ball at the ball park; and it's a long time from baseball season until Christmas. More games have been forfeited by a lost ball than were ever stopped by rain or darkness.

Because most sports editors are from the city, they refer to the sandlots as the place where kids play baseball. But those are city kids.

The country kids play in the backyards and the pastures, where it seems the outfield is always bordered by a crop that is tall and green, or thickly matted.

Sometimes one of my friends had a good pasture where we could set up a field. These are great if they are closely grazed and the cows are gone. The short grass is quite playable, and the cows usually leave a few portable bases around the field.

A good baseball pasture must be grazed short, but not too recently. It's important for the meadow muffins to be dry enough to avoid unnecessary slides or "grandstand plays," as we called them.

If the muffins aren't dry, a player can easily make a couple of hook slides and a dive just between third and home. This is considered showing off — as is catching fly balls while lying on your back.

But this baseball — the one I found in the beans — isn't mine. It belongs to my son. And he didn't even tell me he lost it.

Times have changed. Kids don't hunt them the way we used to. They may have two or three, or figure they'll get a new one.

This sure looks like the one I lost, all those years ago. When I think about how hard I've looked for it, I'm tempted to keep it.

College Education

A hush came over the class as the professor began to speak. "You should have been here last week when that bunch of college students was out here on that agronomy tour. It was the darnedest thing I've ever seen," he said.

He leaned over the bar and continued, "This one kid was betting the others he could bring a dead fly back to life. I wouldn't have believed it if I hadn't seen it."

I should explain, this class wasn't being held in a tavern. It could be called a Center for Continuing Education, or a Sheepherders Institute of Technology. Some would call it a cafe.

It's one of those places out in the farming country, where people come to eat lunch and find out whose combine is broken down, or why the county tore out the bridge. Whatever we call them, these establishments are good for more education per credit hour than any university.

The resident professor also runs the grocery, and meat market, as well as the gas station, cafe and lounge — all in one building. He isn't busy though. The four of us for lunch was the biggest run of the day.

"So this kid poured some beer on a saucer and caught a fly and dropped him in," the lesson continued. "And pretty soon the fly was drowned. Deader than a hammer, apparently.

"Then he got a couple of kids to bet him he couldn't bring the fly back to life," the professor (bartender, cafe owner, storekeeper) said. "And after he gets the bets, the kid puts the fly on another saucer and asks me for a salt shaker. Then he pours about a half teaspoon of salt on top of the fly.

"You should have seen it. Pretty soon that little pile of salt started to rumble and shake, and the fly comes walking out. I suppose he wasn't quite dead or something, or the salt just dried him out; but it was something to see."

"Sounds like it might be a new cure for alcoholism," one of the audience remarked. "You never know what those college kids are going to come up with next."

To me this incident proves the value of a college education. But I recognize that parents send the kids off to college to make something of themselves — and some won't think reviving drunken flies is an important part of the college years.

But it is. One never knows when an ability such as this will prove its value, or when a one-dollar bet may mean the difference between pizza and peanut butter.

I can remember my own departure from the farm in the days when many farm kids didn't have the social conditioning for making a big impression at a major university. Some of us would just stand in the corner when they made us wear neckties to those social gatherings. We always felt like we were tied to something.

And I recall my father's parting words when I went off to college. He said, "Son, I can see that you are the kind of person who is going to make something of himself. But, just remember, if you don't do it too often, most people will forget."

Fuzzy Dogs

Our society is becoming so homogenized there are only a few status symbols left for those who would like to have something a little special. You just can't tell the rich from the poor anymore.

We used to be able to tell something about a person's financial status by what he owned, but you can't even do that now. One of my favorite songs contains the line, "He bought her a big ol' race horse . . . and a funny lookin' little dog."

The song also says, "And he sits in his Jacuzzi and watches the sun go down."

When most of the country still lived on farms, owning a horse wasn't any big thing; and when people had to sit in a tub in the kitchen they would have given anything for a shower. Nowadays everybody wants to take a bath on the porch — and many of them do!

And nobody had those funny lookin' little dogs when we lived in the country. That's because we always had some big dogs for chasing cows and things, and the big dogs would use the little ones for dusters. A fluffy little dog got worn out in a hurry.

Now you can find funny little dogs anywhere, but I still haven't figured our what they're for. Most of them won't even dust without a lot of training.

I've always felt a dog should be good for something. He's got to be big enough to bite a cow, dumb enough to chase rabbits, or ugly enough to scare burglars. A dog has to have a purpose if he's ever going to amount to anything.

A recent visit with some friends reminded me of the thing I dislike most about wooly little pooches: it's their attitude. These dogs are so small that a person tends to ignore their actions, and then the dog develops all sorts of personality defects.

It's the same with kids: Whereas an outsider can tell what's wrong with them immediately, the owners never seem to catch on.

So, we have this curly-haired little dog jumping up and down on the bed and just daring someone to try and stop him. But the owner ignores him! If I had a dog like that I'd put Velcro on the ceiling.

I've always owned dogs that would jump on the bed, but these were bird dogs, and they'd been out in the swamp all day. They just went for the bed to clean up a little.

And they were always sorry. I can't stand a dog that isn't sorry for what he does — one that just dares you to throw him off the bed, or that jumps out of the truck when you tell him to. A truly sorry dog will make you throw him out.

But back to the fuzzy, little pooch my friends have. This dog is kind of special because she can sing. It's true — I saw her do it.

The friend's wife just says, "Peggy, sing! Sing, Peggy!" And then the wife throws her head back and says, "Owoooh! Owoooh! Owoooh!"

And pretty soon the little dog stops jumping on the bed, throws her head back, and says, "Owoo-owooh! Owooooh! Owoo-owooh!" I tell you it's the darnedest thing you ever saw!

I've seen a lot of funny things in my life, but how a fuzzy little dog can teach a woman to sing is surely beyond me.

How to Retire on a Package of Broccoli

Here it is, garden planning time again. Notice I said planning, rather than planting. The successful gardener doesn't rush out and begin planting. He has everything carefully planned out he begins.

The first critical concern of the successful gardener is garden location. This is not as difficult as it may seem, especially if your garden is irrigated. I always just go out and look for the tallest patch of weeds. and this almost always turns out to be the garden. Another favorite trick is to follow the irrigation hose. Nine times out of ten, you'll find the garden at the end of the hose.

Once we have located the garden, most authorities would recommend we make sure other family members know how to find it. This helps give everyone a feeling of involvment in the enterprise, and of course there's always the chance someone may want to go out and pull some weeds, or at least consider it.

I always like to lead family members from the house to the garden at least once a day, until I'm sure they could locate it on their own. Some trainers test more advanced pupils by blindfolding, but I consider this unnecessary.

I am also opposed to the more severe training methods, such as staking-out. I'm always saddened by the sight of a teenager chained to a pickle vine. I just can't get used to it.

While this sort of physical restraint can be effective, I believe it takes away much of the enthusiasm and spontaneity we like to see in a garden helper. These methods should be reserved for those especially difficult pupils who don't respond to persistent shouting and threats of starvation.

The next stage of garden preparation involves the purchase of seeds. This also is not complicated, if you frequent groceries or feed stores and carry a nice wad of money for such occasions.

Nearly all groceries carry a large selection of seeds, conveniently packaged by milligrams. I recently purchased, for instance, a package containing 350 milligrams of broccoli seed.

Because broccoli has small seed, Northrup King was able to put 350 milligrams in an 89¢ package. They have a select group of employees who can perform this feat without laughing.

I bought it. The value was evident. Imagine my surprise when I opened the package to find that a broccoli seed weighs something less than 350 milligrams. There were several in the package!

This, of course, aroused my curiosity to the point of recalling there are one thousand milligrams in a gram and 453 grams in one pound. I had purchased .00077 of a pound of broccoli for 89¢. A quick run through my Oklahoma computer tells me this seed sells for $1155.84 per pound.

Did I plant it? Heck, no! I can't afford to plant it! I'm saving it for retirement.

A New Pair of Farleys

"Who would pay $90 for tennis shoes?" I scoffed. "Farley Moffit would faint if he saw a pair of $90 tennis shoes."

But there they were, top-of-the-line, extra special, NBA style, jet-propelled tennis shoes for $90 a pair. I never thought I'd see the day when tennis shoes were the most expensive thing on the rack.

I remember a time when tennis shoes were the cheapest shoes you could buy, and a person only wore them when he had to. Farley Moffit (not his real name) was the only kid who wore them all of the time the way kids do now.

We laughed at Farley. We'd see some other kid wearing tennis shoes, and say, "Hey, I see you got your 'Farleys' on."

And he'd say, "#@**@#, you #@#-@&X*."

We knew it wasn't nice to make fun of people, but you know how kids are. Little did we know that Farley was thirty years ahead of his time.

In those days most of the farm kids had three pairs of shoes. You had your "Sunday School shoes" which were made of leather, laced up the front, and were cut below the ankles so people could see what color your socks were. These shoes were called Oxfords and only went to Sunday school or the class play. If you wore them to the barn, they would fill up with stuff that made you real obvious at Sunday school (and changed the color of your socks at the same time).

Then you had your clodhoppers, whose purpose was obvious. These were the everyday shoes that got you to school, out to the fields, and chased off the gym floor. They were multi-purpose. Clodhoppers had high tops, big heavy soles, and loop-style shoe-laces so you could get into or out of them in a hurry. The laces were made of something that looked like rawhide or buffalo gut, or whatever was considered tough.

All of these shoes were made of leather. To wear shoes that weren't made of leather was a sign of poverty, or weakness, or a lack of good sense at the least.

Then you had your tennis shoes; and these were ugly. They were not only ugly from the way they were made, but tennis shoes were ugly in a social way, too.

Wearing your tennis shoes to anything more civilized than a locker-room wrestling match was about the most embarrassing thing a person could do. In those days, as today, being embarrassed was right next to being skinned-alive, if you were a teenager.

Tennis shoes were embarrassing because they were cheap. If you wore them to places other than the gym everyone knew those were the only shoes you had. A kid wearing a pair of Redball Jets to the class play would have been the center of attention. His mother would have dragged him out by the shirt collar.

It took them 30 years, but the shoe companies finally figured out what Farley Moffit knew when I was a kid: Tennis shoes were embarrassing because they were cheap. If they were expensive, no one would laugh; and you wouldn't need those stupid Sunday School shoes or those big, ugly clodhoppers. You could get manure all over your tennis shoes, and people would just marvel that you are so rich you can wear $90 shoes out to feed the hogs.

So they made them expensive, and I just can't shake the feeling that Farley is mixed-up in this some way. I'll bet the old rascal has his "Farleys" on, and he's laughing all the way to the bank.

Night League

It seems everyone is studying animal behavior these days. The universities have mobilized the graduate students in an attempt to find out what makes a pig root in the mud, or causes the horse to eat the corral fence.

It has been found, for example, that pigs are happier if they have objects to play with and will spend considerable time playing with these objects rather than fighting with each other. (Sort of like kids, I guess.)

Of course, this is nothing new to any pig farmer who has ever dropped a hat or hammer in the pig pen. Before you can retrieve either object there will be one pig wearing the hat and another pretending he's a carpenter.

The only problem with providing objects for the pigs' entertainment is that you quickly run out of objects. Once the pigs have eaten the hat and chewed the grip off the hammer, most pig owners are reluctant to furnish them with more toys.

However, one of the boys in our 4-H club has solved the problem by providing his pigs with a bowling ball. The pigs like it, it's durable, and it keeps them from fighting.

When I first heard of the bowling-ball idea, it seemed so simple and so effective that I suggested it to my old friend, Howard Smeed, who raises a lot of pigs. You may remember that Howard also traps muskrats, but that's another story.

"Yes, I tried bowling balls with a bunch of pigs a couple of summers ago," Howard said. "But the experience convinced me that I never want to go through that again."

Seeing that he had my attention, Howard continued. "It's too bad, too, because that was a good bunch of pigs. They weighed about 50 pounds when I bought them in April, and I figured they'd be 220 to 240 by August. Then they would be off to market. I was determined to have everything just right.

"There were 100 pigs in the lot, so I went out and bought 25 bowling balls — one for every four pigs, just like the university people were recommending. Everything went fine until about the first of June. The pigs were happy — no fighting — and they were gaining well."

"Then about the middle of June I could see they were becoming more aggressive. There was a lot of squealing and pushing around, and a fight would break out once in a while," he went on. "The fighting and the squealing always seemed to be the worst about dark. So I started leaving the barn lights on for a couple of hours each evening, and that seemed to calm them down.

"Then, I got to watching those pigs more closely, and you know, it was very interesting. One bowling ball was a different color than the others. That's how I first noticed the same four pigs always played with the same ball. Then I realized that the groups of four pigs were always all males or all females — and they never rolled the bowling balls at the same time! The males would roll them in the evening, and the females rolled them in the morning," Howard explained.

"Well, to make a long story short, I lost $2 a head on those pigs, by the time I paid for the feed and the light bill and everything. And on top of that, I got docked four cents a pound on the ones that were overweight when I finally sold them!"

"Wait a minute," I said. "Why was the light bill so high?"

Howard said, "Well, by the end of summer, those pigs had so many leagues, they were still bowling at 2:00 in the morning!"

"And the weight dock?" I asked feebly.

Howard looked shocked. "You wouldn't split up the teams before the summer leagues were over, would you?"

The Migration

Everyone has his favorite signs of approaching spring. For some it's the return of the meadow lark. Others listen for the song of the tree-frog. But for me, spring's nearness is signaled by friends returning from Hawaii, or Mexico, or wherever they went this year.

Their return is like that of the robin, with a hop to the gait and a tan to the belly. They are always so cheerful, like spring itself. I avoid them if I can.

If you, like me, have never been to Hawaii, or Mexico, or Bermuda, you will understand this line of thinking. We just never wanted to go any of those places and run the risk of missing the changing seasons. We crave winter's snowy blanket, the sparkle of icicles on the trees, and pipes frozen in the basement. We wouldn't miss it for anything.

It should be understood, however, there are folks who don't share our environmental sensitivity and will soon be returning from vacations in the bland and monotonous climate of the Caribbean or South Pacific, where they have been frittering away their lives drinking fruit juice and playing golf. These friends will need a certain amount of understanding from those of us who were able to remain behind and revel in our climatic diversity.

We should be thinking of the things we can do to ease the cultural shock for these weary travelers. Of course it would be best to avoid them, but we probably can't. There are too many.

Unfortunately, the colonial practice of putting recent vacationers in stocks is no longer legal. Only a few historians recognize that the earliest use of stocks was for so-called Puritans who spent winter vacations in Florida. This practice permitted the returning vacationer to chat with passers-by, but limited his circulation within the population at large, where his stories were likely to upset most of the wives in the village. This also prevented the returnee from showing a picture of his fish, or girls on the beach, which upset the men of the village.

We should not confuse this technique with the more severe colonial punishment, in which the stockee was fitted with a type of head wrap covering the mouth. This procedure, called "Stocks and Bonds," was reserved for folks heard talking about their vacations and their investments during the same evening.

While the passing of these historic remedies has left us with few alternatives for dealing with the tanned vacationer, we can still be caustic and disagreeable.

We can remember the detrimental effects of sunshine upon the skin, and we can learn to distinguish between a suntan and a volcano burn. We should keep good records; twenty trips to the city equals one trip to Hawaii. If her mother would move to Mexico, maybe we could go down to visit her. It's a lot cheaper to ship that fruit juice and drink it right here at home.

Remember rule 1: avoid them if you can.

The Wagon Man

The best way to get a good rain in this part of the country is to mow some hay down. It works every time.

There are several wheatgrowers around here who have taken to growing a field or two of alfalfa just so they can make it rain when they want it to. They used to go over and try to talk the neighbors into making some hay each time the wheat needed some rain, but that's never quite as effective as cutting your own hay.

I grew up in the East where it rained a lot. We cured hay as fast as the weather would allow, bailed it, and ran for the barn with it.

We pulled a wagon behind the baler, and bales never hit the ground. A man or large boy rode on the wagon and stacked bales as they came out of the baler.

The man on the wagon needed the agility of a circus performer to keep his balance as the wagon lurched across the field. Sudden stops by the kid driving the tractor or a wagon wheel dropping into a woodchuck hole would bring shouts of encouragement from the wagon man. The baler made so much noise that you couldn't hear what he was saying; and judging from his expression, what he said was not fit for children to hear anyway.

Our method of haymaking required considerably more labor than modern methods. We needed a kid to cut the hay, one to rake it, one to drive the tractor on the baler, one to bring empty wagons to the field, someone on the wagon behind the baler, someone to set the hay forks up to the mow, and one to pull the trip rope that dropped the hay and pulled the forks back out of the mow.

There were seven kids in my family, which made labor plentiful. When I consider changes in hay-making methods over the years, I would submit that modern methods have not resulted so much from advances in farm machinery as from better methods of birth control.

Of course haymaking in the West has always been a different sport than we practiced in the East. We used to wait for the dew to dry each morning before baling could begin and usually had to quit by 6:00 P.M. because the hay would begin to take up moisture again.

In much of the West, ranchers bale in the middle of the night to take advantage of the dew and have to quit at 10:00 A.M. because the hay has become too dry.

I look at the expensive machinery we now use to cut, bale, and stack hay and wonder if we've gone too far. The trend toward machines that make large round bales, and the conversion from wire to twine-tie balers, is especially frightening to me.

When I was a kid our bales were all tied with wire, our gates were fastened with wire, and much of the machinery was held together with haywire. (My brother called it twist-type clamps.)

The machinery companies may not know it, but if it weren't for wire-tie balers, most farmers would have to quit. If it weren't for haywire, this whole industry and much of our machinery would fall right down around our knees.

How to Plant a Duck

As this is written, the area remains firmly in the grasp of the monsoon season, and most farmers and gardeners are wondering if the ground will ever dry out for planting. It has been reported that the veterinary clinics have treated several ducks who contracted footrot in wet barnyards.

As we await a drying trend, it may be well to restrain ourselves from tilling soils that are too wet. We must remember the old adage, "If you are wondering whether the soil is too wet to work, you can be sure that it is."

Understandably, the wet winter has brought about some unusual problems. Some have speculated that a mild case of cabin fever is responsible for several new ideas. Others say that the constant drip, drip, drip has begun to take its toll.

The following letters are good examples of recent agricultural concerns.

Dear Mr. Pond:

I have been told that this is a good year for ducks and am eager to grow some. I have had poor luck so far. My first order arrived from the hatchery in

February, and I planted them immediately. My rows were two feet apart, with a twelve-inch spacing within the row.

When the ducks had not emerged after three weeks, I decided that I must have received bad seed and ordered a new batch. Upon the suggestion of my neighbor, I planted the second order in shallow rows with their heads just above the ground. This planting lived several days but grew poorly and finally died.

Do you have any suggestions?

Signed,
Just Ducky

Dear Ducky:

I have little information on growing ducks and can only relate your experience to growing cats. Cats are normally planted in hills. Depth doesn't seem to make much difference but deeper is usually better.

Many people prefer to soak cats overnight before planting, apparently to stimulate germination. It certainly makes them easier to handle. Maybe this would help your ducks. Before planting another batch I would suggest you have your soil tested.

Dear Mr. Pond:

I have done considerable reading on companion planting and stuff like that. I know that beans don't like tomatoes, and rutabagas clash with cauliflower. However, my uncle says broccoli is so temperamental it will leave the garden entirely if it doesn't like where it's planted.

Is this true?

Signed,
Avid Gardener

Dear Avid:

What you have here is a communication problem. (I'll not comment on your uncle, as he is a separate problem). I have nothing against companion planting but would suggest you be more careful in your choice of companions.

It sounds to me as if you also have a general morale problem in the garden, and perhaps all of the vegetables would benefit from counseling. The theories of companion planting have confused some vegetables to the point they are becoming suspicious of their neighbors.

You have no doubt heard potatoes complain that the onions make their eyes water. Petty squabbles such as these should be ignored.

If you can get your broccoli to open up, much of the problem will be solved. Broccoli generally will get along fine with the other vegetables once it realizes that it will not get ahead by leaving.

For many years I have planted vegetables in all sorts of arrangements and configurations. As far as I can tell, the vegetables couldn't care less about their seating arrangement. Of course, I do allow what I call a decent interval between species.

Dear Mr. Pond:

The soil in my garden is still wet. I have considered planting rice, but my wife refuses to pull the plow.

What should I do?

Signed,
Stuck in the Mud

Dear Mr. Mud:

Your questions cannot be answered without more information. For example, how long have you been married? What size is the plow? What size is your wife?

Let's just hope the soil dries out soon. A little sunshine would be good for everyone.

Make Sure He Can't Hear

This week I joined the ranks of the hearing impaired. I woke up one morning, took a shower, and one ear suddenly went dead. Hopefully, it's just a temporary problem with wax clogging or something like that. I'll let the doctor decide.

I recognize that one's sense of hearing is a serious concern, but having none on one side of my head for a few days has had its humorous moments. The experience has given me a better understanding of those fellows who wear hearing aids (as many of us will at some time).

For years I have wondered why the guys with hearing aids are generally such happy, easygoing people. Now I know. We would all feel better if we could turn the world's volume down a couple of notches.

With one ear gone I only hear about half of what's said — which seems to be about the right proportion — and I can pretty much determine which half I want to hear. I listen to all my wife has to say, and simply respond, "Yes Dear," or I don't respond at all. Either way seems to work out fine.

And the kids — I get along great with the kids. My daughter's rock music is much better at half volume. I think I might like that kind of music if I was totally deaf. The vibrations would probably feel good.

Now I understand the pleasant expressions you see on the fellows who can just turn their hearing aid down. They don't hear the little scrapes and screeches that keep the rest of us on edge.

I once knew a fellow who was afflicted with a speech impairment as a young man. He spoke quite clearly, but his speech was about 60 percent profanity and progressed to higher levels as he got older.

Apparently his ears couldn't take it, and he developed a hearing impairment, requiring the use of a hearing aid. This man also had a son who spoke in blue streaks, even as a mere lad, due to the inexhaustible source of material to which he was exposed.

The boy knew his father couldn't hear and would take advantage of the situation to express all sorts of negative opinions about the father, the machinery, and the farm in general.

I helped them bale hay a couple of times, and it was great entertainment. The father would tell the boy to go get him a crescent wrench, and the son would fill the air with curses. He would stalk away mumbling to himself, but he went right over to the tool box and got the wrench.

The boy knew the old man couldn't hear him, and as long as he did as he was told, the verbiage wouldn't get him in trouble. It was a tough situation for an outsider to work in. All you could do was bite your lip, and do your best to keep from laughing.

This man and his son could work together all day without the slightest disagreement. Although many harsh words were spoken, none were ever heard.

One day, while I was sitting in the pickup with the father (and biting my lip), the boy in the back of the truck cut loose with an eloquent critique of his dad's conservative spending habits. His father leaned over to me and said, "He thinks I can't hear him."

Adoption

I knew someone would figure it out sooner or later. There is more money in adoption of animals than there is in raising them.

A farmer in Rhode Island reportedly bought 180 acres complete with a bull and seven cows, and promptly turned the place into a bovine adoption center. Anyone who wants to own a cow can adopt a critter for an initial fee of $250 to $400 and then contribute monthly to help feed the beast.

It's a neat idea — appealing to those with a craving for a large pet, but who don't have facilities for a cow. This certainly makes more sense than the adopt-a-horse program run by the U.S. Bureau of Land Management.

In the BLM's Adopt-A-Horse program they round up all of these wild horses, then require people to pay a fee in order to take a horse home with them. This eliminates folks who really care about horses, but who don't have a barn and hay stack.

Some would say comparing the Adopt-A-Cow plan with the BLM's adoption program proves the superiority of private enterprise over public management. If Congress would allow the BLM to follow the Rhode Island farmer's plan, people could adopt these wild horses and then just pay for their keep out on the range.

Now I know some will say the purpose of the wild horse adoption program is to get the horses off the range; but that's being narrow-minded. The man in Rhode Island has only 180 acres, and is offering to keep these cows as long as the owner can support them (for a fee of course).

This fellow is not dumb, either. He permits the owner to have his cow slaughtered if the owner so decides.

I figure if the BLM would charge a fee for adopting a horse, and a second fee for maintaining these horses on the range, most owners would opt for doggie biscuits sooner or later.

This would allow those who can afford these horses to help support them in their wild and unfettered state, and the rest of us could adopt a cow or a pig — whatever we like.

The man in Rhode Island gives the adoptive parents a framed color photo of their cow, and the family is entitled to hold a party on the farm each year to celebrate the cow's birthday.

It could work the same way with wild horses and burros. It's possible to get a picture of most of them, and there's plenty of room for birthday parties out there in the rimrocks.

The horses wouldn't have to be identified real carefully, either. If someone wanted to see his horse, he could just take the picture out and try to match one up.

The plan reminds me of the two farm boys who each received a pig for doing chores around the farm. The father put both pigs in a pen and told the boys to take care of them, and they could have the income when the pigs were sold.

The younger son was really proud of his pig, although he wasn't yet sure which was his. So he asked his brother, "Which pig do you want?"

The older boy said, "Oh, it doesn't matter. We'll just feed them together. They're both about the same."

The younger son had some difficulty with this and nearly every day would ask, "Which pig is mine?"

The older said, "Oh, it doesn't matter. They're both good pigs."

Then one day one of the pigs died; and the older brother broke the news to the younger. "I'm sorry to tell you this, James, but I'm afraid your pig just died."

Aesop of the Eighties

The grasshopper plague is back in many parts of the country, and the hoppers are sure taking a beating in the newspapers. Nearly every day you can read that eight grasshoppers eat as much as one cow, or that forty acres of grasshoppers will eat the entire farm before breakfast.

Some of these figures are not entirely accurate, but it has been proven that an outbreak of grasshoppers can lead to distortion of the memory.

It's easy to hate a grasshopper and we should all feel free to do so. This particular insect is totally irresponsible and without principles. He would just as soon eat your best begonia as look at it.

But even with all of his destructive tendencies you have to appreciate the way the grasshopper looks at the situation. The hopper really doesn't mean anyone harm (as long as he gets enough to eat of course).

I think the best way to understand grasshoppers is to recall the story of the grasshopper and the ant. As I remember the story, there was this grasshopper who spent the whole summer playing golf, letting his yard go to seed, and generally making a spectacle of himself. But he was having a good time.

Everyone hated him for this, especially the ant who ran the local shoe shop and never had time for golf, except for an occasional outing on Saturday mornings. But the ant was in good physical shape and kept his waistline down by jogging to the store each morning.

So by the end of the summer the grasshopper had practiced his chipping and putting until he was down to a 12 handicap, while his friend the ant could barely break 100 (even though he played winter rules all summer). This was most discouraging to the ant, who developed an unfriendly face and began to scurry around his store with hardly a kind word for anyone.

Finally, along about September the evenings began to cool and the grasshopper began to dub his tee shots. At first he didn't know what to think and tried to blame it on the cold weather. But the pro told him it looked more like a case of the yips (or maybe the yumps in his case).

To make a long story short, his handicap shot up into the late teens and he began to spend more time in the clubhouse looking at new clubs. And it wasn't long until the ant began to beat him on the short par threes, and the hopper got so stiff he had to hire a beetle to carry his clubs. The other bugs were beginning to talk about the hopper's poor physical condition, and his wife was putting iron pills in his juice.

Then one day the grasshopper hit his tee shot out-of-bounds on number three, and the ant couldn't resist lecturing him about his unhealthy lifestyle, not to mention his vocabulary. The ant (who had just turned 40) told him about the new exercise program he was on and how much his physique had improved since he began jogging every morning.

Then as they stood on the tee box talking, a big grey seagull swooped down and sucked them both up.

You are free to put your own moral to this story. For me it says, "It only takes a couple of hours to play nine holes."

Happy Chickens

It seems to me a lot of that talk about alternative agriculture has died down the last few years. I know the concept is still alive and active in some circles, but I just don't hear as much about it these days.

A few years back there were alternatives galore. There were so many alternative crops, alternative animals, and alternative lifestyles you couldn't tell the straight farmers from the alternates.

I had people bringing me books stating that wheat was a permanent crop: if you harvest it by hand and spill a lot on the ground, it will volunteer back so you won't have to plant it again. These books said if you had a cow and a handful of seeds, you were self-sufficient.

The author of one said you should pen the chickens close to the house, and the deer in the next pasture, and the wallabies way out in the back forty. None of these animals has to be fed because they are all natural.

You would not believe what some of these folks were suggesting. The crops and the animals were so exotic a guy would have to learn three languages just to cuss the cows.

One of the big selling points for some of the alternative ideas was the success people had with them in faraway places, such as India. I think many of the alternatives lost a lot of following when people actually tried them — and found that water buffalo chips are so much more expensive than ammonia sulfate.

I've always thought we should be careful about interpreting and adapting foreign agricultural practices, unless we know exactly what we're getting into.

About a year ago my wife and I were hosts for a farm tour to Europe and, like others in the group, were at the mercy of our very knowledgeable and charming tour guide. She knew her history and her cultures, but I'm not so sure about the stories she told about European agriculture.

They may have been true, but how can one tell?

For instance, our guide said there are two kinds of chickens in European countries, such as her native Switzerland. One type of chicken is raised in a pen and called a "factory chicken", and the other variety runs loose and is called a "happy chicken."

She reported that people pay twice as much for happy chickens at the store because they are better to eat, and the same is true for eggs from happy chickens (called happy eggs, I suppose). And we saw them from the tour bus — happy chickens everywhere, running around the yards, digging up the flowers, and thumbing their beaks at Colonel Sanders.

There may be some validity to these chickens being happy, and I suspect their owners are happy, too. We have one happy chicken at our place, and it surely has fun around the shrubbery and the flower beds. I've named it "Noodle Soup" — just to keep it from becoming totally hysterical.

We could probably learn something from the Swiss about raising happy animals. My kids' sheep would be a good example. We keep them fenced in, but not so tightly they can't get out and have a good time once in a while.

This concept of happy sheep makes me feel better too, because I don't have to keep fixing the fence like those people with the factory sheep. It gives one a whole new outlook on the livestock business.

Don't Eat the Avocados

I learned many years ago that the field of home economics is more complicated than most of us realize. I learned this both from my wife, who is a home economist, and from my many years experience in county extension offices.

The home economist has to handle everything from soup to nuts — and from the most conservative homemaker to the most rabid feminist. The field is both large and heavily mined.

I can well remember those times when the home economist was out of the extension office, and we had a person on the phone with a canner full of beans and a somewhat cavalier attitude about botulism. There were a few sweaty moments.

It was with mixed emotions that I read of a recent university study which proved that people often make faulty judgments in determining food safety, tending to discard food too soon as a result. This is contrary to all I ever knew about food safety.

When I worked for universities we generally took the position that all food was basically unsafe, and the sooner you threw it out the better. I always took the conservative position on such matters.

People would call and say, "I have these apples I canned, and I wondered whether . . ."

I would say, "The home economist is gone, but we recommend you throw the apples out and destroy the jars. Yes, the wide mouths and the narrows — throw them away!"

If they said the freezer was off, and the meat had started to thaw, I said, "You should throw out the meat and the freezer, but it's probably O.K. to keep the house."

"Trash-and-Burn" was my motto.

The food safety experts say most foods should be safe if kept below 40° F. or over 165° F. But I never could figure out how to get anything from 165° down to 40° without passing through that unsafe area in between. You might just as well throw it out.

The recent study found one of the most common mistakes made by families surveyed was over-reliance on package dates in deciding when to discard foods. Some folks said they had heard food should never be kept in the refrigerator more than three days.

The researchers also found people discarded perfectly good avocados and dark-skinned muskmelons as being over-ripe.

I'm not surprised by any of these findings. I discard avocados wherever I find them, just as a matter of principle. The same with muskmelons — one whiff and they're gone.

At our house anything over three days old probably does have something wrong with it. If the kids haven't eaten it in three days, it's considered a hazardous substance. You may as well trash it.

I think the safety researchers began their study with the misconception that the refrigerator is a food storage device. Maybe it is in some places, but not at my house.

At my house, we see the fridge as a place one goes to look for food. Sort of an agreed upon gathering place. (It makes a good sign board, too.)

I think of the fridge as a food safety testing device, rather than a safe storage area. If I put something in there, and it's still there the next day, I'm suspicious.

If it's not gone in three days, I bury it.

Pasture Pool

Golf has become a popular sport in both rural and urban areas. This is a healthy trend, I think, and should reduce the snide remarks commonly hurled at those with a compulsion for "pasture pool."

Even though golf is becoming a sport of the masses, the game still maintains a certain intimidation for those of us who don't score in low numbers. We can't shake the feeling that a little Scotsman with a gnarled stick would probably beat us in a fair match.

This inferior attitude is further encouraged by those who frequent country clubs and insist on wearing funny little hats. Even our greatest shots and highest accomplishments are demeaned by the unreasonable goals set by others.

Those who speak about "birdies" or strive to shoot a score equivalent to their age must be ignored if the average golfer is to have any self-respect. For years my goal has been to score lower than my body temperature.

I agree with the man who said, "No man has truly mastered golf until he realizes that his good shots are accidents and his bad shots are good exercise."

That's one reason I can't go along with the latest trend of having golf clubs designed to fit your swing. A club that holds your head down and keeps your left knee from buckling must take a lot of fun out of the game.

I read a daily newspaper which publishes the names of everyone who scores a hole-in-one. In a section called "Scoreboard" I see that Hank Swatch made a hole-in-one on the 165 yard ninth hole at Pleasant Hills. He did it with a seven iron. His eighth hole-in-one in 20 years of golfing.

This is just the sort of thing that ruins the game for me. If I ever make a hole-in-one, I certainly won't tell the newspaper. How would it look?

"Roger Pond made a hole-in-one on the 120-yard fourth hole, using his driver — his first hole-in-one in many years of golf (he can't remember how many). After his ball bounced off a tree and rolled into the cup, he ran from the green shouting, 'But it still counts, don't it?' "

One of the prime tools of those striving for status on the golf course is the dress code. I recently played at a country club where designer jeans are listed as a requirement for male golfers.

"My son asked, "Are Levis designer jeans?"

"They were when I was your age," I replied.

It was fun to compare that club's dress code with accepted dress for the course where I usually play. The club we visited requires male golfers to wear designer jeans and shirts with a collar, whereas our club requires that a shirt and shoes be worn at all times.

We don't even require pants! But I guess some things are understood. Golfers should retain a certain amount of dignity, even if they do kick their ball from the trap occasionally.

It may be hard for youngsters to accept a dress code requiring that shorts have legs of a certain length, or that men golfers must wear shirts. But someday these kids will be old enough to make the rules; and then they, too, will realize there is nothing more disgusting than a young golfer with his flat stomach showing.

Bringing Home the Bacon

Big-time advertising is getting a firmer grip on the farmer's dollar. The dairy people have a head start when it comes to media advertising, but the beef producers and pork producers have recently taken the plunge.

The National Pork Producers Council announced a campaign to promote pork as "the other white meat," in an effort to slice into the chicken market. They hired Peggy Fleming, former Olympic gold medal winning figure skater, to help show what pork can do for the body.

One report says the industry is also considering changes at the retail level, such as relabeling ham as "fresh pork rump roast." That's O.K., with me. I don't care what they call it, as long as it tastes like ham.

I like ham and bacon and probably won't shy away from fresh pork rump roast, if it doesn't take longer to say it than it does to eat it. I am real partial to bacon; and because I like the flavor, I depend upon bacon grease for cooking certain things.

I know the nutritionists will caution against using animal fats for cooking; but I grew up that way, and I need it for fry-ing things like eggs or venison. This has never been a problem for me, because all of the bacon I buy at the store has plenty of grease.

This fall, however, we bought a pig from one of the kids in the 4-H club. It was an underweight pig that didn't get big enough for the county fair. At only 180 pounds, this animal made very good pork, but the bacon is so lean it doesn't make any extra grease for cooking.

So the other day I went to the store to get some grease. I walked boldly up to the meat case with only one mission: Get my bacon grease and get out of there before some nutritionist tried to sell me chicken.

I was starved for bacon grease. It's hard to describe the feeling: After all of these years of rooting through the meat case looking for lean bacon, now I was after fat!

It was easy. I just grabbed the first package I saw. If we could average the bacon in the case with what I have in the freezer, we would have pretty good meat.

For $1.79 I got 12 ounces of bacon containing 8 ounces of grease. I threw it in my cart and went for the checkout. Now I have a supply of bacon grease to last me all winter, and it only cost $1.79.

I always try to learn from these little experiences. If consumers like me are used to buying bacon that leaves lots of grease, maybe somebody should relabel the bacon.

Call it "fresh pork cooking grease." Or how about "extra lean animal oil"?

I know someone will tell me about the lean hogs produced on farms today, as compared to those old fat ones we used to have. But as a consumer, all I know is what I see in the meat case.

It's not the grocer's fault, either. Somebody is selling him that bacon.

If I were a pork producer, I would cheer when Peggy Fleming skates out there to tell everyone about the "other white meat" and its new, lean image. But I would also skate on down to the packing house and the grocery to take a hard look at what's going into the meat case.

Hay Buyer's Dictionary

This is the time of year when cows and cowmen begin to look at the haystack with the gnawing and certain suspicion that it's not big enough. When the cows can see over the hay stack, they become understandably nervous.

Of course, some people never seem to run out of hay, but these are not my kind of people. They are the ones with good tires on all of their vehicles, gloves for both hands, and a tractor that starts when they push a button. I'm not talking about them. I'm talking about the rest of us.

Buying hay doesn't have to be a traumatic experience, but it can be. While buyers and sellers generally can count on fair treatment, there have been instances of communication breakdown.

I have identified the major cause of bad experiences in hay buying and selling and have taken it upon myself to solve the problem. My new pocket dictionary of hay description is guaranteed to clear up nearly any misunderstanding that may occur from communication breakdown. Owners of this handy reference are almost sure to amaze their friends and surprise their neighbors.

The *Dictionary of Hay Description* recognizes that both buyers and sellers attach subtle meaning to the common terms of hay description, and therefore I list terms in both languages: buyer's and seller's. The following is a sample.

Green Leafy: Buyer
Green -as in St. Patrick, color of "go" light, and of pine trees (live ones).
Leafy-1) made up of leaves, 2) devoid of stems, example: lettuce

Green Leafy: Seller
Green-1) color of all hay, 2) a plant once capable of photosynthesis, 3) a tint sometimes seen when hay is held toward the light.
Leafy-1) had leaves during the current growing season, 2) bales pull apart in flakes (as in leaves of a book), 3)past tense: descriptive of a former condition.

Small Stemmed: Buyer
1) No stem larger than horse hair. 2) Can be slept on in the nude, comfortably.

Small Stemmed: Seller
1) Not suitable for heavy construction. 2) Some stems O.K. for rafters, a few for fence braces. 3) Bales do not flake (leaf), must be cut with chain saw.

Little Bloom: Buyer
1) Occasional flower found in a truck load of hay. 2) Singular: for example-one "little bloom" in entire field.

Little Bloom: Seller
1) Similar to mountain meadow in May. 2) Less color than Japanese Gardens. 3) Haystack reflects purple in sunlight. 4) Blooms are little.

Dairy Quality: Buyer

1) Preferred food of discriminating cows. 2) Must be moved quickly or hay will convert to milk in the stack.

Dairy Quality: Seller

1) Can be slept on by dairy cows. 2) Eaten readily if no other feed is provided for several weeks.

Feeder Hay: Buyer

1) Good for feeding. 2) Not quite as good as dairy quality.

Feeder Hay: Seller

1) Suitable for heavy construction, such as building feeders. 2) Sometimes pronounced "Feed'er", meaning you can feed'er use for firewood, either one.

Stemmy: Buyer

1) Hay that grows on stems. 2) Leaves grow some distance above ground, rather then sprouting from the surface as mushrooms do. 3) Pajamas required for sleeping.

Stemmy: Seller

1) "Dunt understanda deh woid."

This handy reference is available to you free of charge, if you send one self-addressed, stamped envelope and one-half bale of hay (green leafy) to this address. Hay will be refused if it is in the envelope.

Leave the Kids Alone

There's nothing like the pressure-cooker of high school sports to build character in a person. An important game can test the physical endurance and mental toughness of the most seasoned fan.

A big game must be tough for the players, too; but it's the fans that are most likely to come unravelled. The players have a coach to tell them what to do, and they have practiced all week. They are hardened to the pressure.

But the fans come out cold. All we have is a hard board to sit on and the foggy memories of our playing days to remind us that we had a hard board to sit on in those days, too. It's really difficult to sit there quietly and let the kids play their game.

What's even harder for me is to sit in the stands and listen to folks yell at the referees. I've seen referees do some pretty crazy things, but I almost never yell at them. I just can't think of anything to say.

Another reason I don't yell is the fear that some day a referee will hand me his whistle and ask me to go out there and try it myself. A lot of folks would be quieter if they thought about that for awhile.

I recently attended a basketball tournament where some of the fans got a little over-enthused with the referees. This was an AAU event for 14-year-olds and under, where several teams and their fans converged for a weekend of basketball.

One of the early games was less than half over when someone decided the referees were playing favorites. Things went down hill from there.

I did learn a few standard phrases to use when hollering at the refs. When the referee blew his whistle, one fellow yelled, "Come on, ref! Let the kids play." A few minutes later the ref didn't blow the whistle, and the same guy screamed, "You're gonna get someone hurt out there!"

This group of fans badgered the refs, yelled at the kids, and one fellow began shouting plays to the team on the floor. I've always figured it's hard enough to give the kids good advice if you are the coach; it's even harder if you're not.

I was reminded of an incident described by a county agent friend who judges livestock shows. My friend, Ken, says he was judging a beef cattle show some years back, when he noticed one boy kept glancing toward the side of the show ring.

The young man had a well-fitted animal and obviously knew something about showing cattle, or had received a lot of help from someone. The kid was doing his best but seemed a little nervous.

Pretty soon Ken could see that the boy's mother was standing on one side of the ring and giving him instructions each time she could get his attention. Then Ken noticed an older sister was on the other side of the ring, giving more suggestions each time the boy got close to her.

The young man was getting frazzled, and Ken was about to put a stop to all of this sideline coaching. But by then the boy had progressed to the side of the ring near his sister — and she said something to him.

The boy turned to his sister and said, "Ah-h-h, shut-up!!"

Under his breath Ken said, "A-a-a-men."

Barn Office

I have always thought a person's office should be an extension of his personality. The office should be stimulating. It should generate ideas.

If you are a sheep farmer, your office should have baby lambs in the corner and a window overlooking the pasture. A corn grower's office needs some combine sprockets for paper weights, or a bag of seed on the cabinet.

An office needs this kind of atmosphere to keep in touch with the basic elements of the business. I keep a few sheep penned in the barn below my office, just to remind me of what I'll be doing if this column doesn't sell.

Some people have found working out of their home is not as easy as it sounds. I can tell you that working out of your barn is no piece of cake, either.

The barn office is like a woodlot. If it isn't managed, it will soon revert to wilderness. My office is in continual transition between a hay mow and a machine shop. If left alone this place would be full of straw bales and anvils in a matter of days.

One problem with an office in the barn is keeping the animals from getting involved in the business. The large animals can be excluded by closing the door, but reptiles and other small vertebrates are another matter.

One day this fall, I found a very dry tree frog under a large telephone book. He may have been looking for a number, but I don't see how he could dial one if he found it.

This frog had put himself under a lot of pressure. By the time I found him, he was just another bookmark.

Then this week, I turned on my computer and a bug walked out of the disk drive. I watched as the insect emerged, starry-eyed, and walked across the desk and under a manila folder.

Then I recognized this as one of those "sage bugs" people used to bring into the county extension office. I developed a special fondness for this species when I was a county agent. It was one of the few insects I could identify.

The entomologists call them sage bugs because they smell like sage if you mash them. The folks who find them in their house call them a lot of things, because they stagger across the bathroom counters and fall into the sink.

I thought about calling the extension office to ask about controlling sage bugs in my computer but thought better of it. In my office, I figure anything that doesn't chew gum or try to edit my writing is pretty much harmless.

Then I realized a beetle in a computer disk-drive is no ordinary insect. With 128K of random access memory and full IBM compatibility this bug might be dangerous.

The next day the beetle came staggering out of the computer again, his wings bent and his eyes glassed-over; he had the look of one who has been up all night writing. Each time the computer came on, the bug's eyes would light up, and he would jump on the keyboard as if he had something to say.

If the beetle had written his own stuff, I would have let him go; but when he started fooling with mine, I had to use the phone book on him.

My Equipment is Killing Me

The fall hunting seasons have always been a time of excitement for me. I can remember as a boy going to bed early the night before the opening of squirrel season, and then lying awake for hours listening for the wind in the trees near the window.

Wind was bad for squirrel hunting because it took away the chance of hearing the squirrels chomping on nuts or rustling about the trees. We always prayed for a windless morning on opening day.

As I look back I can see that my values have become twisted with age, and today I probably wouldn't shoot a squirrel for anything less than a personal insult. I have gone on to bigger game.

It is my theory that hunters progress through a series of predictable stages from their early experience in the quest of squirrels and rabbits to the more strenuous foray in pursuit of deer, elk, or bear. And with each stage they acquire some new equipment.

The young squirrel hunter can make do with the hand-me-down 22 rifle, but as he goes after progressively bigger game his equipment list expands to include the 4x4 truck (with winch), several high caliber rifles, tents, stoves, camp coolers, spotting scope, and a number of other essentials a younger mind might not think of.

With thisequipment, the more mature hunter is capable of launching one major expedition each year in search of the biggest creatures listed in the hunting booklet. He is no longer tied to hunting close to home with only the shirt on his back to protect him from the elements.

And the mature hunter has developed a creed of sportsmanship that makes the trip far more important than the bagging of game. This creed serves him well, because he hasn't killed anything for a long time.

But he is well-equipped if something should come along. He is prepared to skin it, quarter it, pack it out, cut and wrap, cook with any number of tasty recipes, and take pictures of the whole operation. Someday he will, too.

This fall's elk hunt taught me the value of adequate equipment. I had it all with me: tent, stove, grub box, rifle, cooler, lantern, cot, sleeping bag, saws, shovels, ropes, etc., etc. And after about a day's work the camp was up, and I was set to go hunting.

I should explain that I don't go with an outfitter, as some hunters do. I'm too independent for that. I'm also too poor for that. (I think those two traits are carried on the same chromosome.)

After setting up camp and carrying all of that equipment around, I was reminded of the aging hunter's fate. Just about the time a man gets all of the equipment he really needs, he has grown too old to carry it around.

A man's last hunting trips are a sad thing. He typically gathers all of the family around his bedside. He asks them to assemble all of his equipment there in the room. Then he says, "Could you folks please help me carry this stuff to the car?"

Truckers Welcome

I should have known when I saw the sign stating, "Under new management. Truckers welcome." The previous owner must have gone broke or was run out of town, and the truckers didn't feel welcome for some reason.

A sign like that is a dead giveaway. Everybody knows truckers don't care if they're welcome or not, as long as the food is good. (Did you ever see a sign saying, "truckers not welcome"?)

But I walked by the sign without even thinking and sat down on a stool at the end of the counter. I was in a hurry and ordered apple pie and coffee.

What could be more American than apple pie and coffee? Well, I'll tell you straight away this wasn't an American apple pie: This was about the most foreign piece of cookery I have ever seen.

This pie was floating around the saucer in some sort of liquid I assume dripped from the refrigeration unit. The crust was soggy. The apples were soggy. It was kind of like pie ala moat.

But I was in a hurry and began to eat it as best I could, when I heard a woman's voice in the kitchen say, "I hope we make some money at lunch time, 'cause I got to buy some Pine Sol and see if I can get rid of that smell."

I began to think, "I'm having enough trouble trying to get this pie down without hearing about any smells in the kitchen."

So then she comes out of the kitchen and stands at the end of the counter and says, "Boy, that's the awfulest smell I ever seen. Have you ever smelled a skunk up close like that? You know when you go by one on the road, you just git a whiff, but up close they smell just awful!"

The other customer was finished eating, and I suppose he was listening, but I couldn't look up. Sometimes it's best to mind your own business.

"My dog got into it with a skunk this morning; and, boy, did he get nailed!" she continued. "My boyfriend heard the awfulest racket out in the yard and ran out to break it up, and that skunk squirted the dog right in the face just as he got there. And Frank came running back in the house with the dog right behind him and before I could slam the door, he ran in and rubbed his face all over the rug."

"Who? Frank?" I asked.

"No. The dog," she said. "And now I got to git some Pine Sol or something to git rid of that smell. You can put tomato juice on a dog, but you can't do that with a rug."

"How about Frank?" I thought. But I really didn't want to get in any deeper.

"I don't know how I'm gonna git rid of that smell," she went on, as I paid my bill.

"And how about Frank?" I thought again.

The bill for that apple pie float and a lousy cup of coffee was $1.80. It was worth it though: I did get a column out of it.

The Boz vs. Don Eagle

I have always said fashions will repeat themselves. That's why I kept all of my narrow ties until they came back in vogue. When something goes out of style, I simply put it away and wait for the next wave.

So I wasn't surprised last fall to see the new haircuts on college football players. I knew they would come back. The basic "Don Eagle" we used to call it. Now it's "The Boz"; but it's the same thing.

Don Eagle was a wrestler. The Boz is a linebacker: Same thing.

It's different now, though, because lots of kids are getting Bozs. When you got a Don Eagle you also got a school vacation, because they threw you out until the hair grew back.

You couldn't get a small town barber to give you a Don Eagle. They would agree to a flat-top or a bur, but they always gave you whatever they thought was best.

We had three barbers in our town, and they all worked in the same shop. This gave a person a certain amount of choice on who cut your hair, but it wasn't easy to get what you wanted.

Our barbers were Willie, Benny, and Jack — and each had a style of his own. Jack was a young guy who stood about six-feet-seven and had to scrunch down to sight across your flat-top to see if it was level.

He had to jack up the chair as high as it would go in order to reach the shorter kids. Then he had to jack it back down when he was finished, so the kids didn't break a leg jumping out of the chair.

Jack was good on flat-tops, because he broke into the barber game about the time they became popular. Willie and Benny were used to giving burs. Their flat-top always had a hump in the middle.

There was a long bench down one side of the barber shop where you would sit and read comic books until it was your turn. Then, you would have to ask for the barber you wanted.

This was the hard part, because you didn't want to hurt anyone's feelings; but if Benny's or Willie's chair came open, you would have to say, "I'm waiting for Jack."

This didn't seem to bother the barbers much, but I aways felt sorry for Willie. He was such a nice old guy you hated to pass on his chair, but you knew he would round off your flat-top or put a ditch down one side or something. You just couldn't take a chance.

This wasn't Willie's fault, either. He had a wooden leg on one side that was about half-an-inch longer than his good leg. Several times during a haircut, Willie would swing the wooden leg around and rest his weight on it. This put him a half-inch higher than he was on his good leg, and it affected his haircuts.

You could look in the mirror and tell which side of your head was cut while Willie was on his pine leg. The other side would taper-off with about a six percent grade. Later in the day when he got tired he would shift several times — giving your hair a windrowed effect.

I would try Benny once in a while, but he was risky, too. Benny was bald, and all the kids said he wanted us to look like him. He gave a mean bur that seemed to last forever. Benny saved the parents a lot of money.

Willie and Benny are both gone, now; but I expect Jack is still cutting away. He's probably giving out Boz's, and I'll bet they're still flat across the top.

Bed and Forget-the-Breakfast

One can learn a lot about the motel business in rural areas by just looking around and reading signs in the rooms. It's enough to make a person nervous.

Signs like "Please do not clean birds in the room," or "Do not water horses in the duck pond," give a vague idea of what the small-town motel operator is up against. But if you think that's scary, consider what's in store for some of these new bed and breakfast establishments.

Bed and breakfast may be the inn thing in some parts of the country, but I'm not sure American culture is ready for it. To me, bed and breakfast sounds like something one does to relatives. I would never have the nerve to try it on a stranger.

It may sound like fun to get to know one's guests personally, and share bathrooms and all that; but I think we should give the whole thing a little more thought.

People traveling through most rural areas are going hunting, or they may be headed for the next rodeo. They aren't the same clientele the tourist areas are used to.

I'm not being negative. I'm just saying we need to take a look at our travelers before we decide to launch a bed and breakfast business.

Let's not go tripping through the house shouting, "Tennis anyone?" when the parking area is obviously full of cattle trucks. And if we serve a continental breakfast to those cowboys, they won't even know they've eaten.

Let's consider what time do we serve breakfast for a bunch of goose hunters? And must they wear a shirt if it is covered with blood from yesterday's hunt?

How many birds will your freezer hold? Or do you have a place a guy can hang a deer, so he can skin it out?

If old Gunsmoke breaks his chain and gets a couple of ducks off the pond, does the guest pay for them, or do we cook 'em up for dinner?

The small-town motels have been down this road before and have learned to deal with travelers of all sorts. A few may have become a bit defensive as a result.

I stopped at a motel a while back and was standing in the lobby, waiting to check in. Two men registering at the desk were obviously traveling on business, as I was. One of them asked, "Are there phones in the rooms?"

The woman behind the desk said, in a rather nasty tone, "Phone calls are 50 cents."

The businessman said, "But I'll be putting them on my credit card."

"All phone calls are 50 cents," she straightened him up again.

By now she had his attention, and his jaws clamped down like a vise. There were no more frivolous questions from this gentleman until I later saw him in the parking lot, and he asked, "Is this the only motel in town?"

Looking at it from the traveler's side, I'm sure some will welcome the bed and breakfast concept as a way to get better acquainted with their host. Others may just want a telephone, a key to the room, and a real good lock on the door.

Class Reunion

Well, we finally did it: My high school class has scheduled a reunion for this summer.

This may not sound like much to many readers, but it's pretty special for my old classmates. You see this is our 25th reunion, but it's also our first. We never had one before.

Attending the class reunion sounds like fun, but unfortunately I'm going to miss it. There are a number of reasons for my absence, mostly related to distance and time.

It might seem that 25 years is a long time to wait before planning a class reunion, but my class has grounds for delay. We left high school like a covey of quail flushed from a fencerow, and most of us have found a good hiding place. We're hunkered down pretty low.

When we left the auditorium at graduation, there were only a few classmates who didn't break and run for the door. In his speech at graduation, the principal said, "When one of you kids becomes successful, you ought to have yerselves a reunion and talk about it." I guess someone must have finally made it.

Actually, there were a number of potentially successful people in my class. Several were selected to attend the military academy at Fort Leonardwood, Missouri. A couple of others went to Yale and visited relatives.

A few of my old classmates have gone on to become doctors and ministers. I remember the tricks these guys used to pull in high school. That's why I try to avoid attending church or getting sick in that part of the country.

I can see now that waiting 25 years before having a reunion probably isn't a good idea. Most of us have reached that point where we can hardly remember high school, let alone the people with whom we shared the experience.

I'm afraid that for many classmates the years have melted together until high school has become a mere lump in the pudding. Some of us have gone to other class reunions, and had a pretty good time until we found out it wasn't our class — that's why everyone looked so young.

Even if we still have our mental marbles in the bag after 25 years, a person has to face the physical realities, too. A lot of potatoes have passed through the skillet since graduation day.

My son fell into a panic one recent Sunday because his seventh-grade class was scheduled to go swimming on Monday. He needed a swimsuit, and the stores are closed on Sunday.

While he was frantically calling friends to borrow a suit, I suddenly remembered my old suit was downstairs in the dresser — the swimsuit I wore in high school.

The old swimsuit fits the seventh-grader perfectly. That's just one more reason I can't go to the reunion. My swimsuit has apparently shrunk something awful.

Its Hard to Look Cool When
Your Car's Full of Sheep

I used to envy the people who have the right equipment for whatever job is at hand, but not anymore. I have learned to enjoy the challenge, break new ground, express my ingenuity — and basically scrounge around with whatever I have.

For example, most people who own livestock have a truck for hauling their animals. But these people don't learn anything. It's no big deal to haul animals in a truck — anybody can do that.

If you really want to learn about animals, you should haul them in a station wagon, or the trunk of a Pontiac, or in the back of a Scout like I do. This way you learn how a pig reacts to being tied up in a sack, and how far a sheep can jump with its head stuck in a panel and a kid hanging onto one leg. It's amazing!

Just recently some friends called to get advice on getting pigs into their van so they could haul them to the county fairgrounds. Unfortunately, I was out hauling my kids' sheep in the Scout, but my wife knew what to do.

She said, "Get the pig into a corner, and put a bucket over his head so he can't see where he's going. Then you can back him in."

The friends used a pillow case instead, and it worked great. When the lights went out, the pigs just went limp. They thought it was a kidnapping.

A person can learn a lot from the animals in the back seat. These critters have heard about the market, and they're saying, "Oh, no. Not this little piggy! I'd rather be in Philadelphia."

There are a few principles to remember when hauling animals in the car. First, allow extra time. It always takes a little longer when you have to catch each animal twice, wrestle them to a draw, and then drive down the road with a sheep breathing down your neck.

Second, you must remain calm. Jumping, shouting, or pounding your fist on the barn causes unnecessary stress for the animals. It's best to go about your business quietly.

Third, don't let on that you have a pig in the back of your car. Naturally, everyone can see that you do, but less than one percent will suggest there is anything unusual about hauling animals in this way.

This is because most folks are afraid to say anything. They suspect you might be dangerous.

They are correct, of course. After fighting with a 200 pound pig for most of the morning, one may not be in the best of humor. Such a person might very well use heavy objects to express himself.

Last, but not least, try to appear confident. Consider this an everyday event. You just load up the sheep and take a little drive down to the fairgrounds. But don't stop at the grocery!

Air Jerry

How about that Spud Webb, sports fans! What a hero for the small player!

Now, wait a minute. I know what you non-sports fans are thinking. You're going to say Spud Webb is how a spider gets his potatoes, but we're gonna ignore that.

Spud Webb is the 5 foot 7 inch basketball player who won the NBA slam dunk contest. And he did it without ladders, hay bales, or any other climbing device, save some type of booster rockets no one has yet been able to catch him with.

Spud Webb is from Texas. He's what Pecos Bill would have been if Bill was raised by jack rabbits instead of wolves. Old Bill would have been a point guard in the NBA, making a lot more money than he ever did rodeoing.

Never in the history of basketball has one so small been able to get up so high. Only once have I seen anyone put more air under him than Spud did in the slam dunk contest. It wasn't on TV and I was the only witness, but I can still see ol' Jerry sailing through the air ten feet above everything, hollering things his mother wouldn't like, and scattering cows as he went.

I should explain Jerry was the neighbor boy several years my senior, and he would challenge me to a little one-on-one when there was nobody else around to play with. The only time I could stay with him was in the fall when our court in the hay mow was still narrowed to about 8 feet. With hay on one side and the wall on the other, my opponent had to take the ball out-of-bounds and dribble around me to get to the basket.

Although I was younger and a lot smaller, I could be pretty tough in that narrow space. I would operate like a late model Hoover every time the ball hit the floor. Jerry quickly learned that dribbling was dangerous, and we didn't allow shooting from out-of-bounds.

Then one day, Jerry developed his play. He would throw the ball over my head, run around me to catch it on the first bounce, and then make a layup. You have to be fast to throw the inbounds pass to yourself, but Jerry was fast. (Everyone said he could turn off the light and then jump in bed before it got dark.)

His play worked fine on a dry floor. It had rained this particular day, however, and the wooden floor of the court was wet where rain blew through a hole over a door under the basket.

The door under the basket was used for throwing hay out of the mow and down to the cows. It was about four feet wide and latched with a hook. I would estimate the hay bales leaving that door made a drop of about 10 feet.

So Jerry had the ball out-of-bounds at the back of the court. He made the high inbounds pass and raced past me, heading for the basket. Catching the ball on the first bounce and running full speed, Jerry leaped in the air for the lay-in and came down in the wet spot on the floor.

His feet came unglued, and he hit the door at full speed, the latch broke loose and Jerry was airborne out over the barnlot. He didn't know what was below, and I couldn't have told him. But we were lucky. The hay manger had been moved, the mud and manure was about 2 feet deep, and the cows, thinking he was some type of giant eagle, cleared out when they saw his shadow overhead.

I ran to the door and realized that Jerry had left the arena before the ball went through the basket. Maybe I could disqualify the points because the shooter wasn't present. But how could he know if he made it?

"You missed!" I shouted.

Shearing Sheep

At first I thought he was kidding — a joke. It had to be a joke. Could he come over and watch me shear the sheep?

No one watches me shear sheep, at least not anymore. My kids watched the first time, but they are older and wiser now. Only the other sheep watch the shearing these days, and they aren't likely to tell any stories.

My friend was serious, however. He actually wanted to watch. "I need to shear ours, and I've never done it before. I figure a person can always learn something by watching others," he said.

That's true I thought: A person can learn something at a lynching, too, but that doesn't mean he ought to go to them!

"I am the world's worst sheep shearer," I pleaded. "You are surely welcome to watch, but it's likely to be messy."

Maybe I was exaggerating a little: No one can say for sure who is the worst sheep shearer. Most of the competitions are for the best.

I am really pretty careful not to cut the sheep, though. My blood-and-gore stories are designed to frighten people away more than anything.

My daughter and son helped me shear our first sheep several years ago. Laura was nine and helped by holding the shearing chart so I could see where to make the cuts (a term used loosely to describe direction of movement for the shears). Russell was five and helped by climbing 15 feet up an oak tree and then falling out just as I was starting on the second sheep.

Between the daughter's laughing and shouts of "O-h-h-h, gross!", and the boy's need for a long nap, that wasn't one of my better days.

Since then, I've shorn the sheep alone; and I do what I can to maintain the solemnness of the occasion. The sheep know the rules. The first one to laugh is going to be next, and nobody leaves the barn until the wool is in the bag.

My friend was serious about watching, however, and arrived as I was trying to tighten the screws on the shearing comb. The sheep were running in and out of the barn, practicing for the main event.

Terry quickly sensed that I was a bundle of optimism. "I'll show you the way I shear sheep, and then you'll know what not to do," I told him.

"The Mexican shearers used to tie all four legs together, but I just tie two. I figure that gives the sheep and me an equal chance," I explained.

Then I went to work on the smallest ewe. Terry accused me of shearing that ewe first because she is the smallest and easiest to handle. I denied that assessment but failed to tell him she is also the oldest and least valuable.

In a little over an hour, I had shorn the whole flock, which is pretty good for me. People who have more than three sheep may take longer — or shear faster.

. Terry was really very helpful and pointed out the proper techniques, as they are explained on the shearing chart. We found the wool comes off much smoother if a person follows directions.

As I finished the first ewe, Terry said, "I don't think that's a bad job at all. I think she looks pretty good."

The ewe said, "Bah!." But then, I've always said a sheep has little appreciation for anything.

Don't Use the Seat

It was just a simple trip to the bank. But there were a few complications: The bank is four miles away, my wife had the car for the day, and the second car was at the repair shop.

The temperature hovered between Bake and Broil. My ten-year-old son was trying to talk me out of it. "You'll kill yourself," he said. "You can't ride that thing."

"Watch me," was my confident reply. "Just show me how to shift the gears. Why do they put the handle bars on upside down? When I was a boy, you didn't have to lie on your belly to ride a bicycle."

"Why don't you just call someone and borrow their car? You're gonna crash for sure," was his confident reply. "These are the brakes, and here's the thing you pull down to make it pedal easier. But you probably won't need that — you'll crash for sure."

"Never mind about the brakes. I'm only going to stop once. The bank has some nice shrubs. They'll stop me."

"They call this a bicycle? The whole thing is tin foil and plastic. They call these tires? No wonder nobody rides this thing. I'll be back about 5:30 or 6:00. You stay in the house and keep cool."

"You'll be back in a few days, or whenever they let you out of the hospital," the boy groused.

But I made it — into town, accomplished my business, and back — all in the allotted time. The fool thing tried to throw me a couple of times, but I think I taught it a lesson or two. I think I'll walk next time.

If you've ridden a bicycle since 1960, you may share my grief for what has happened to this noble beast. They've been bred for racing and for show to the point where they are no longer fit for riding.

The handle bars are located under the critter's chin, where you have to reach down and grab at them. It's like riding a horse without bridle or reins, and holding a stick in his mouth with both hands, instead. And this animal never lifts its head!

So there you are, clear up over the neck of this pile of aluminum tubing, and they have built you a seat just a few inches above where the withers should be. This seat is shaped like an oblong saddle horn and is just slightly smaller. (You won't use it if you're smart.)

Then they put some brakes on these new bikes, along with about eighteen gears. The brakes are better than putting your foot in the spokes, but far less reliable.

To work the brakes, you pull a handle that pulls a wire, causing a stick to rub against the tire. They were designed by an engineer.

The gears allow you to switch back and forth between speeds to feel like you're doing something. This has something to do with not being shiftless, but I don't have time to figure it out.

Now I read that the bicycle companies are getting into what they call "mountain bikes." These have the handle bars above the ears, wide tires so you can ride off the sidewalk if you want, and a seat that you can sit down on. We had bikes like these years ago — before people had to have special pants and crash helmets to ride a bicycle.

Tell It Like It Is

Ah-h, yes, here it is: my seed catalog, printed, mailed and received with boundless optimism. Few books permit a more complete escape from reality than the seed catalog.

Everything in the catalog grows. I have yet to see a case of blight or a wimpy, little potato in the seed catalog. Everything is big and juicy, delicious to eat, and easy to grow.

And I believe them! Every year, I believe them! Just once, I would like to see an honest seed catalog: one with more accurate descriptions of what's going to happen in my garden.

My version of a seed catalog would tell it like it is. People would cry when they read it, but some folks like that sort of thing.

If you, too, have been disappointed by traditional seed catalogs, the following vegetables can be ordered from me direct. They aren't pretty, but they're honest.

Big, Long Carrots 70 days (and nights)

One of our most popular veggies. Probably won't grow in your garden. (Your soil is too hard, and your back is too weak.) Many gardeners plant these just for fun and exercise. A favorite with moles and rabbits.

Super-Burp Cucumbers (Excuse me)

Great for those summer salads. Some folks plant them for when relatives visit. Will grow in the most difficult soils, or in the seed package if shipped in warm weather. Be sure to point the package away from you when opening.

Big Red Tomatoes 30 days (Suspended)

Our shortest season tomato. Can be planted anywhere south of the north pole, although they won't necessarily produce fruit. Many growers like to plant Big Reds in pots and take them to Florida for ripening. Beautiful vines.

No Fooling Garlic 90 days (no nights)

The family-planning vegetable. We have good reports from all over about this variety. Mrs. (name withheld) from Westport, Kentucky writes,"I have nine kids, and growing enough vegetables for this crowd is a big chore. Since I started using your new garlic variety, I found out what's causing it."

Miss Susan's Blackeyed Peas 80 days

Our most insulting vegetable. One of the few plants that prefers shade over sunlight. (Probably to reduce the shine.) Seeds should be planted in single rows some distance from other vegetables, and out of earshot if possible.

Chinese Peas 60 days

One of the most ornamental plants we sell. Goes well in salads, stir-fry, and nearly any type of ornamental cooking.

Early Glacier Sweet Corn 80 days (in most climates)

A real favorite in the North because of its hardiness. Some growers report planting it in the spring and harvesting in the fall of the same year. Mrs. Harold Smith writes from Uphome, Wisconsin, "Please send three pounds of Early Glacier. We have a difficult time getting good sweet corn up here, and that is about the best corn we ever ate. Leave it on the cob this time. My husband likes it better that way."

Uncle Ed's Horse Nuggets

Here's an easy way to make all of your plants grow faster. Plant one or two nuggets in each hill, and jump back before you get your eyes poked out! Some growers plant several nuggets in each hill, just to amaze their neighbors. In Texas, they plant the whole horse. (Uncle Ed says it's actually cheaper than producing the nuggets.)

Progress

I would expect that many older cattlemen and women are amazed at the progress that has been made in beef cattle breeding over the years. These folks can remember the days when commercial cattle herds often contained a composite of several breeds. Cattle in these herds were mostly this and part that. They were identified more by what they looked like than by what they actually were. Texas longhorns, for example, just happened to be cattle with long horns.

Through years of education and application of proven genetic research, cattlemen were encouraged to upgrade their herds by using good quality purebred bulls. Progressive cattlemen took to this idea readily, and soon nearly all of the good beef cattle herds in the country were made up of the three English breeds: Hereford, Angus, and Shorthorn. By continued selection these herds were brought to a high standard of excellence. Changes in the standard over the years may have confused things some, but at least the cattleman had something to shoot at.

There were, of course, a few less progressive cattlemen who continued to cross breeds and refer to Herefords as "white faces." These cattlemen were soundly ridiculed by more progressive ranchers, and crossbred cattle were generally called "scrubs." Records indicate this ridicule didn't bother the cattle so much as it did the cattlemen.

After most herds in the western half of the country were purebred Herefords, and cattlemen had developed nice uniform cattle that seemed to do well on the range, somebody at or near a university announced that a 15% increase in many productive traits could be obtained by crossing the breeds together. Through the phenomenon of heterosis it was found offspring of two breed crosses perform better than the average of the two parents.

This caused many progressive owners of purebred herds to laugh. The less progressive cattleman, who still had his scrubs, just sort of chortled.

It took many years to convince owners of purebred cattle that crossbreeding was the progressive thing to do. These folks had been progressive when they developed their quality purebred cattle, and it wasn't easy to de-progress them, so to speak.

Over the years, however, crossbreeding of Angus, Herefords, and Shorthorn cattle became quite common. Black cattle with white faces became the mark of a well-planned crossbreeding program, rather than evidence of poor fences.

Good planning has always been emphasized in crossbreeding programs, and cattlemen were strongly advised to use good quality purebred bulls. Evidence that the crossbreeding program is well-planned separates the progressive cattleman from the less progressive cattleman. The industry has taken a lesson from the government here, and agrees that almost anything you do is O.K. as long as you planned to do it.

It is true that some less progressive cattlemen have continued to use bulls of many different breeds (including crossbred bulls), and now have herds made up of five or six breeds. On the other hand, some more progressive producers have started using longhorn bulls purchased from less progressive cattlemen who kept them around all these years.

This brings us to the present. Scientists at the USDA Beef Cattle Research Center in Nebraska are breeding cattle to produce three new composite breeds called Marc I, Marc II, and Marc III. The Marc I, for example, is composed of one-fourth each Charolais, Brown Swiss, Limousin, and one-eighth each Hereford and Angus.

I should point out that this is entirely different than the less progressive breeders who have mixed-up their herds through a poorly-planned crossbreeding program. These scientists planned to do this.

Older cattlemen (those over 1,000 years old) may remember that most of our breeds of cattle were originally developed this way. However, it was difficult to get many breeds together in those days because of transportation problems. This was before the invention of the wheel. I can hear some of the less progressive cattlemen start to chuckle at this. Now cut that out, you guys!

Who'll Buy the Cats?

It's easy to see that U.S. farm programs are becoming more complicated every day. The modern farmer has become a government program analyst in addition to all of the other things he does to keep a farm going.

Farm programs are a terrific source of frustration if one thinks about them too much. Right now, farmers need government programs to survive, but there is the nagging memory that most of the farmer's current problems have resulted from someone trying to help.

I am thankful there are few government assistance programs for writers. Something like that would put me out of business within six months. Every day I write my congressman saying, "Do whatever you guys do in D.C., but please don't try to help me!"

It's probably too late for farmers to plead for less help, but some of the new farm programs are enough to make one wonder. Consider the Dairy Termination Program, for example.

The Dairy Termination Program is designed to get rid of dairy cows (and dairy farmers) through a herd buyout program for those willing to sell their herd and swear they won't milk cows for five years. The idea is to reduce the milk surplus, which should help the remaining dairy farmers.

Some people think this program should require participating dairymen to attend weekly meetings, so they won't slip up and buy more cows. Each farmer could be assigned a buddy to call when he had the urge to buy some cows, and the buddy would try to talk him out of it.

This may sound strange, but we have to understand what we are dealing with here. These are people who get out of bed at 5:00 A.M. seven days a week, 365 days a year, to go out and milk cows. Then they go back to the barn each evening and do it again.

I grew up on a dairy farm, and I've seen how these guys get started. My brothers did the milking at our place, and two of them became dairy farmers. They always said they could quit if they wanted to, but neither of them has. It's a terrible habit.

They all start the same way — it's a social thing at first. You go out to milk, and your friends from town are out there chatting with you. You squirt milk at the cats, and everybody has a good time. It just seems the thing to do.

Then one day you find you're doing it alone. You don't have anyone to talk to, so you start talking to the cows. After a while it's the money: You don't have any, and you know a few more cows are all you need to make it big.

By the time a guy reaches middle age, it's too late. You're gonna wake up at 5:00 A.M., anyway; You might as well be milking cows.

Maybe there are dairymen who want to quit, but they sure don't show it. Most of us would have quit every morning at 5:00 A.M.

Maybe the Dairy Program will have a few takers, but I figure every dairyman in the country is just watching and hoping the other dairy farmers will sell out to the Feds.

It's a way of life for a man and wife,
Though the kids are grown and gone.
We could sell the cows,
We could sell the house,
But we'll still wake up at dawn.

Little Brothers

There is an ancient proverb which says, "Give a man a fish and you have fed him for a day. Teach a man to fish, and you have fed him for a lifetime."

Obviously this is an old proverb. Fishing just isn't that profitable anymore, but I suppose the concept is still correct.

My earliest experiences were after fishing had become a sport, but before you had to throw everything back. In those days before spinning reels eliminated backlashes, fishing was a mixture of sport and work.

The sport has changed. Now we have bass boats and fish-finders and all sorts of gadgets. I saw an ad recently for a computer unit which attaches to your rod and registers a strike. The computer tells you how much the fish weighs, the proper amount of drag, and how long the fish fought before it was landed.

I could have used one of these the time I caught my brother Kenny's ear with my streamer fly. I guessed he weighed about 150 pounds, dragged me 50 feet, and fought about 10 minutes; but I suppose a computer would have been more accurate.

Kenny taught me how to fish in the little farm ponds common to the part of the country where I grew up. He taught by example. After I had watched him cast for a few hours, he would let me put the worms on his hook and take the fish off if he caught any.

That was an era when everyone had a brother. You never got to do anything until you had watched your brother for awhile. By then it was usually dark and you hoped for a chance the next day. I had three older brothers and became a very restless spectator.

My brothers got new rods and reels when I was just big enough to foul things up real good. I still remember the day they bought those fancy glass rods from the local hardware store.

The store owner took hold of each end of the rod and bent it over double to show how flexible it was; and then he waved it around like a bull fighter going in for the kill. If the store had been full of bulls they would have all been slaughtered.

We were impressed and bought two rods and two "Green Hornet" baitcasting reels. Green Hornets were the top of the line at our hardware store. It was the only kind they had, anyway.

Of course, all of this fancy equipment was for my bigger brothers, but I was watching. I could see myself casting from one side of the pond to the other and yanking out those bass like they write about in the magazines: The ones that look like milk cans on the bottom of the lake.

But you didn't just go out and start fishing with those baitcasting reels. It took some practice in the back yard to learn how hard you needed to cast to clear the milkhouse roof and how much spool tension would reduce the incidence of backlashes. These reels had more bird's nests than an Audubon magazine.

I became an expert on bird's nests. A slight foul-up would produce a wad of line looking like the dwelling of a small wren. Casting to the far side of the pond would produce a structure suitable for a pair of young orioles.

When a kid gets a backlash like this with his big brother's reel, he goes through several predictable stages. First there is panic while he tries to untangle it. Then, there is the urge to hide it. And lastly, he denies it ever happened: "What reel? How would I know? The cat probably got into it."

All of This Will Be Yours and the Bank's

The media has discovered the farm problem, wrestled it to the ground, and is painfully twisting its arm. If there is any problem with farming that we haven't read about, it will surely be in tomorrow's paper.

There have always been problems in farming, but they didn't often get much press. But now the financial laundry is being hung out to dry.

I can remember when the farm problem first began. It was back about a generation ago when Dad first sat down beside one of the boys and said, "Son, this will all be yours someday."

And the boy said, "Man, you have been out in the sun too long! If you think I'm gonna milk those cows for the rest of my life, somebody must be putting weeds in your tobacco."

Of course Dad was startled by this reply; but he later sat down beside one of the other boys and said, "Son, someday all of this will be yours . . . and I'll throw in the machinery and half the cows, with no interest for the first five years."

And finally, he found one who wanted to be a farmer. This was one of the better boys, too — hard working and a smart kid — but still he wanted to be a farmer.

So, all across the country these young men were getting started in farming. And most of them did real well.

Some worked hard and made good management decisions and they succeeded. Others worked hard and made bad management decisions, and they succeeded, too.

This was hard for the banker to understand, but he got caught up in the whole thing and loaned everybody lots of money, figuring hard work must be good for something.

It was about this time that we got economists, and they were saying you've got to get bigger and more efficient. Now they're saying you need to get smaller and more efficient. (At least they're consistent on the efficient part.)

The economists said you shouldn't be afraid to borrow money. They talked about leverage and things most of us didn't know much about. Some people suspected the economists didn't know much about them either, but nobody could prove it.

Then the chickens came home, and it was evident they were planning to roost. Farm prices were bad, and then they got worse; and the interest rates got steeper than a cow's face. The economy turned off sour, and with all this money borrowed we could see we had a farm problem.

I don't know whom we should blame for the fix agriculture got itself into. The government didn't help matters any with the high interest rates, and embargoes, and reports that prosperity was on the horizon. The bankers couldn't really help themselves, and the economists didn't see the grease on the rail, either.

I don't think we should blame it on Dad, either. He was doing the best he could.

However, in the future when we sit down with one of the boys, we might say, "Son, someday your brother will probably be farming this place for the bank and couple of highrollers; and if you would like to become a lawyer, I'm sure he would appreciate it."

An Honest Tan

Where I grew up a "redneck" was a person with an uneven suntan. Only his neck was red, because a hat protected his head and the shirt collar was snugged-up to exclude dust and chaff.

Now we have a different class of people with suntans, and these aren't rednecks. These are The Young and Handsome, who have been lying around in tanning booths to acquire a smooth and silky tan formerly associated with a perfectly toasted marshmallow.

These people want to look tan without having to chop the wood or sit on a tractor all day the way folks used to get their sunshine. Somehow those artificial tans never look quite right to me: They are too soft and mellow.

I figure a good honest suntan can only be acquired through outdoor activity — preferably through useful work (or fishing). When I was a boy, we got tan by driving the tractor. If I had been a girl, it might have been a little different; but many of them got tan working outdoors the same as the boys did.

We boys would just yank off our shirts each spring, and in a few days we were tan. The girls had to be a little more careful; but the girls who were assigned to driving tractor would do everything but stand up and drive backwards to get as even a tan as possible. They were hard on fences sometimes.

When we got tan it was with pure sunshine — none of this artificial light and fancy tanning lotion. Maybe I should take that back. Our tans were mostly sun, but some extra substances were involved, too.

These other substances were incidental materials — not suntan lotion. In those days, a boy caught out in the field smearing on suntan lotion would have been laughed out of the country.

Things like dust and oil, bearing grease, or horse sweat may also enhance a tan; but everyone saw these as natural substances. Besides, no one used these lotions on purpose.

Some of the best suntans I ever had came from working ground with my brother's old John Deere B tractor. Those who drove the old John Deeres will remember they were two-cylinder jobs, fondly labeled as "two-bangers."

And they were! You could hear these tractors for miles, "Ker-Pow, pow, pow-pow-pow." This particular old B had a problem with some cylinder rings or something, and got into the habit of spraying small drops of unburned gasoline and oil out the exhaust. Every "pow" contained a few drops.

You may remember, too, that the exhaust was above the engine and directly in front of the driver. And tractors didn't have cabs like they do now. After a full day of tractor-driving, the kid would come in pretty well oiled.

It was great for suntans, though. A guy could take off his shirt with full confidence that several hours from now he would be brown as a berry; and along with the sunshine, the oil and gasoline spray produced a deeper, smoother tan than you will ever see come out of a tanning booth.

And best of all, there was no embarrassment with this kind of tan. It wasn't like today, where you have people going into tanning booths and hoping to get out the back door so the people in the coffee shop won't see them leave.

The Pond Camp

The summer at Grandpa's farm holds fond memories for many adults of my generation. Of course a trip to the farm still generates memories for youngsters today, but there aren't as many Grandpas with farms as there used to be.

The kids are not the only ones with memories of summers in the country. Aunts, uncles, grandpas, grandmas and cousins have their memories, too — even though these recollections may not match up exactly.

While a trip to the country is nearly always a fun experience, a lot depends upon preparation by the host. Our three-year-old niece who will be traveling with her grandmother to visit us this summer might be a good example.

While the child's mother writes that Erica is perfectly behaved, she mentions that the swelling in the little girl's hand has not yet subsided from the last time she got it stuck in a gumball machine.

We are preparing for the visit.

When I was a kid and cousins came to visit our farm, we were always well-prepared. Our farm was like a summer camp. There were seven kids in the family to begin with, and a few visiting cousins just added a little more life to the party.

The arrival of relatives meant there were now enough for two softball teams. And when things got dull we could always dare each other to do those things no one would have tried without a large audience.

Then, there was always some educating to be done. It was somehow important to convince the town kids that brown cows give chocolate milk and that you can tell bulls from cows by the length of their horns.

Of course, the city cousins were just as smart as those from a farm, but they knew they were out of their element. You had to feel a little sorry for the kids who were transferred across societal lines without the needed preparation.

It worked the same way when we went to visit relatives in the city. There was no way for a country kid to determine what was acceptable behavior in the city — and all the town kids knew it. They would cook up the darnedest schemes.

Writing "Get out of town by sundown" on playing cards and leaving them on people's door steps was probably not a good idea; but how is a country kid to know his cousin is just looking for a little excitement? The police seemed to understand.

One of the big adjustments for kids visiting in the city was the difference in eating habits. People in town often had access to a larger variety of foods and seemed intent upon springing something new for each meal. This was tough for a kid who thought meat, milk, bread, and potatoes were the four food groups.

Most of us handled it pretty well, but one country cousin finally broke down during a summer visit. He was used to eating three square meals a day (with two or three round ones in between); and he just couldn't stomach the more exotic vegetables.

After a few days, my aunt gave the boys some money for the swimming pool, and Frank siezed the opportunity. As soon as they were out of sight he told his younger cousin, "If you think we're spending this on swimming, you're crazy. We're going to the grocery. This is for food!"

Don't Sniff the Livestock Books

I have long been a collector of government bulletins. I can go to my bookshelf right now and tell you when to wean baby goats I don't have and how to fertilize 18 crops that I have never seen. The bulletins are always handy and well worn.

Until recently this kind of information wasn't available in books; but it was only last week that I learned why information on goats, hogs, and fertilizer is best suited to bulletins rather than traditional-style books.

A friend who works at the library told me, "We always have to check the livestock books when they're returned. They usually have hay and manure in them. Do people read them in the barn?" Then she laughed, "Ha, Ha."

But I didn't laugh. I remembered my booklet on how to bone out a deer and the blood that took out page 19. And I thought of my sheep shearing chart with the jagged edge where the clippers got a bit too close.

I considered the times I have loaned veterinary books to friends and then tried to diagnose their animals' ailments by the spots in the book when it was returned.

Obviously, there is much to be learned about the proper use of books about livestock. We should first acknowledge the problem is with the inexperienced livestock producer. The old pros don't read books in the barn.

The experienced producer knows that reading books makes the animals nervous. They have already decided you don't know what you are doing, and seeing you reading books merely aggravates this suspicion.

Sometimes the animals can be put at ease by showing them the cover photos and reading a few pages to them. In general though, animals have little interest in literature and couldn't care less about photography.

About the only time I use a book in the barn anymore is for disease diagnosis or treatment. For example, I have found the small paperback of 80 pages or less can be useful in treating ruminant bloat.

The booklet is simply rolled into a cylinder and tied at both ends with baling twine. This is then tied crosswise in the animal's mouth to encourage belching. Some farmers use a piece of broomstick for this, but a small book will work fine.

This important element of book design is often overlooked by authors of livestock books. An eight-by-ten booklet also makes a good funnel and can be used for up to three drenches if the cover is fairly slick.

The larger hardbacks are obviously not much good for funnels or gags but are often better for disease diagnosis. Because they last longer, hardbacks can be taken right into the pens with the animals and will often come out in pretty good shape.

I have one large veterinary book that has diagnosed dozens of diseases and probably cured countless animals. Because of its size the book is also good for getting a critter's attention, if it refuses to accept the prescribed treatment.

My method of diagnosis is not complicated. I simply take the big veterinary book into the pen and look at the pictures until I find one resembling the animal in question. Then I take the same book to my veterinarian and ask him to guess what disease the animal has.

Usually the vet will ask a few questions, such as whether the animal has scours, or if there is any bloody discharge. The book really helps here, too; because I can say, "Yeah, I think there's some stuff back here on page 46. This is pretty bad, isn't it?"

The More Things Change

For many high school seniors and their parents this is a time for important decisions about college. May we all survive this period of delicate negotiations between the generations.

There are bound to be little disagreements about college: Things like whether parents should help pay tuition, absorb all college expenses, or merely purchase the college of their choice.

Going to college has changed since the days when I left the farm, driving my father's '54 Chevy and carrying a wad of traveler's checks in $10 denominations for paying tuition.

In those days the tuition at Ohio State University was $100 and was promptly paid by signing over 10 of my traveler's checks. Tuition there is probably higher today, as it is at other universities my daughter expresses interest in.

Laura says all of the students on campus have cars, and most of them also have a small motor scooter to get around between classes. She thinks she will need a scooter very soon.

I suggested she talk to the students who have both a car and a scooter to see about borrowing the scooter when they are using the car. It makes little sense for everyone to own all of this transportation.

Many of us had cars in my college days during the early '60's, but our cars were a primitive lot. Manual transmission or power-glide were about the only options available. And four-on-the-floor was often more descriptive of the passengers than a particular type of gear shift.

Several years later major college campuses were closed to vehicles during the peace riots. Many students accused the alumni of organizing the riots, just to get rid of the cars.

Today's students have a few more needs than we had. They need a stereo and a microwave oven, and no one can get by for very long without a television. Now, they have to rent a truck to haul their stuff to college.

One of the big factors in selection of a college these days is location of the campus. That was true when I went to school, too. I drove around for over an hour before I finally found the campus.

Now the kids look for a college that is close to the ski slopes, and of course they need oceans for surfing, and perhaps a city where they can get away for a few days when school work gets too hectic. The college must offer a good education, too, and lots of dances.

Looking back, I don't suppose I would have gone to college if I couldn't go home and hunt pheasants; so maybe kids haven't changed all that much.

I remember sitting next to one of my animal science professors at a banquet for college seniors who were receiving scholarships in the college of agriculture. It was two days before Thanksgiving, and I had plans to leave school a day early to get in an extra day of hunting over the holidays.

Why I told the professor I was going home a day early to spend Wednesday hunting is beyond me. Perhaps the devil made me do it.

Professor Wilson said, "But you can go hunting on Thursday."

"Yes, I'll go then, too," I replied.

I don't know how my classmates did on Wednesday's pop quiz, but I know how I did. Now that I think about it, I guess professors haven't changed all that much, either.

Your Traditions, Or Mine?

The Christmas season is recognized across America as a time of religious celebration and great traditional value. Even the incipient intrusion of commercial interests cannot dim the strong family traditions of this season.

We find that Christmas traditions are as varied as the ethnic, religious, and economic diversity that make up this great nation. Unfortunately for many families these traditions are not well defined.

Sometimes through the uncertainties of matrimony two people are brought together without regard to differences in ethnic backround, religion, or Christmas traditions. And there are still those hard-core conservatives who believe what God has joined together will have to tough it out.

As a result, we have families who don't agree on what their traditions are. This creates consternation, conversation, and (hopefully) compromise.

For example, if your family always opened presents on Christmas Eve, and hers always opened theirs on Christmas morning, an immediate divorce may not be necessary. Why not open them in the middle of the night — say 3:00 A.M.?

Or you could take turns. One year the family opens presents on Christmas Eve, and the next year all presents are opened Christmas morning. (In this case, she owes me 20 years.)

In cases of extreme stubborness it might help to open one present per hour beginning about 9:00 P.M. The beginning time can be adjusted to allow completion before breakfast.

Even more serious than disagreement on family traditions is not having family traditions. But this is not a major obstacle, as every magazine with *Country* in the name is loaded with stories about family traditions. It's a simple matter to pick out whatever activity appeals to you.

A second alternative is to make up your own family traditions. This works best if you have young children or a brand new wife. (Older children won't believe you, and few wives are that new.)

I try to make up a few old traditions each year depending upon the weather, financial constraints, and work I need to do. Last year I helped my son crack hazelnuts for roasting in the open fire (oven). This is one of those old family traditions that began when I got the hazelnuts and has been discontinued now that the nuts are gone.

In years when we have a white Christmas I remember the old family tradition of shoveling snow on Christmas day. When I want to go duck hunting my old memories again come winging through the fog.

I like to tell the kids about the things my family used to do on Christmas day. Things like feeding the hogs after we all ate breakfast. I keep these memories alive by helping the kids place corn cobs under the Christmas tree.

We should remember that the holidays can be a time of sadness for those who are unable to observe their traditions. The person who always goes skiing on New Year's is devastated if there's not enough snow. The Ohio State alum feels like buzzard bait when Iowa goes to the Rose Bowl.

But such traumas can also be mitigated. The skier can get out his skateboard and jump off the roof, and he can get someone to jump on his leg and try to break it. The Ohio State alum just has to suffer — unless he can find a skier from Iowa.

Don't Buy the Cute One

O.K., I guess we'll have to do it. It's time to take the kids out to the farm to select their 4-H projects. While this may sound like fun to some folks, the thought brings twitches to the jaw of anyone who has been through it. Picking a project animal is no big deal to the kids; but for the parents, it can be a terror.

Over the years, I've discovered several techniques for reducing the anxiety surrounding this event. Although each method has its penalties, these few suggestions may provide aid and comfort to parents who are new to the game, or who may be naive enough to believe last year was not typical, i.e., it couldn't happen again. Believe me, it won't happen again in quite the same way, but it will happen again, somehow.

Obviously, the best way to reduce hassles in animal selection is to leave the kids at home. Unfortunately, this idea has several drawbacks, such as recurring waves of guilt, accompanied by the certain knowledge the kids will tell everyone in their club, and half of those people attending the County Fair, that they were home watching TV when the animals were selected. You will have to take them along. They will enjoy swinging on the hay rope, while you look at the animals.

An alternative would be for the parents to stay home, but this isn't practical, as we are needed for transportation. I've tried swinging on the hay rope, myself, while the kids look at the animals; but this has its problems, too. Although I can occupy the rope and keep the kids away from it, this trick is sometimes mistaken for a suicide attempt; thereby drawing more attention than I would like.

If we take the hard-line approach, as we should, and make the kids select their own project animal, several precautions should be taken. First, we should lecture the youngsters during the trip to the farm to be sure they will pick a good animal. Tell them to look for size and scale, length of loin, and spring of rib in breeding stock. Discuss the importance of good muscling and trim appearance in market stock.

But don't be too surprised if the kids don't assimilate the entire lecture, or are less than perfect in their terminology. If the youngster wants to buy a pig "with a big rear" that's O.K. with me, as long as he doesn't say I told him to. If he just gets one that walks normal and doesn't wheeze, I'll be happy!

Upon arrival at the farm, the alert parent will do whatever is necessary to get to the barn first. If there are any cute, little, scrawny animals with floppy ears in there, get rid of them. I don't care how you do it, but get rid of them. The kids will select these pitiful critters from a herd of thousands.

If you are buying steers, be wary of those that seem exceptionally alert. (The ones with their head in the air and their nostrils emitting little puffs of smoke.) These steers will have a tendency to wander. They'll wander up your chest and down your back, through the garden, and just about anywhere they want to go. You will see them at the Fair with two log chains around the neck and two men holding onto each chain. These steers are hazardous to your health.

On the other hand, if you just can't take the strain of selecting project animals, you might want to raise your own stock. Then selection is easy, but the rest of the year is a complete circus.

A Litter of Biscuits

Urban migrants moving into rural communities are sometimes concerned about how they are accepted by neighbors who seem to have arrived with the pioneers. It's a difficult question, but not a serious problem, really.

As one who grew up in a rural area and has lived in similar communities most of my adult life, I have never had the slightest concern about whether I was accepted by the oldtimers. I figure they have to accept me. I'm a fact of life. They don't have to like me, but denying I exist is of no benefit to anyone.

So, one becomes a new neighbor who has just moved in, or a new person who has been there 20 years. But they have to accept you.

A friend in a rural community once told me about being introduced to a long-time resident, who said, "Oh, yes, you're the new people who run the drycleaners." This was true — she and her husband had owned the drycleaners for 22 years.

One can be new for a long time in some places. That's the difference between small towns and cities. In the rural community, if they haven't met you, you're new.

Rural people expect that newcomers won't be around long. It takes time to form lasting friendships in a farm community. Folks who are only going to be around for a generation or two don't really have time to get acquainted.

Farm people actually like newcomers, but they know established residents are more predictable. The locals know who drives down the middle of the road and whose dog eats chickens. But newcomers are an unknown quantity. They upset the balance.

It's hard to make a big impression in farm communities. Positions don't count for much. It doesn't matter that you are president of the Downtown Garden Club — we know your beans will wilt like everybody elses.

Rural communities will accept people for what they are, but they don't give any slack. If one plans to become an established family, he should bring a lunch and a bedroll. It's going to take awhile.

Readers may have heard about the young school teacher from Cleveland who moved to a small town in Maine and was wondering how soon he would be accepted as an established member of the community.

After about ten years of residence, the teacher said to a neighboring farmer, "You know, I understand that I will always be an outsider in Maine. It takes a long time to become established in an old community like this. But how about my kids? They were born here. Will they be accepted as bonafide natives?"

The old-timer kicked around in the dirt a little bit and finally asked, "You have a cat don't you, Jim?"

Jim said, "Yes, we have a cat."

"Let's look at it this way," the farmer said. "If your cat had kittens in the oven, you wouldn't call them biscuits, would you?"

Beware of Animals

"Well, his tail is a little crooked, and look at his head: He's got Woody Woodpecker's head. Where did you say it was made?" I chortled.

"What do you expect for eight dollars?" my wife returned fire. "I really like it. The tag says it was made in the Republic of Maldives. Maybe they have a different kind of pheasant."

That's a new one on me. The Republic of Maldives? Maybe they do have strange pheasants.

I looked at the sweater a little more closely and sure enough, the bird on the front is a dead wringer for Woody Woodpecker in formal attire. I would have mistaken him for a pheasant if it weren't for that silly grin on his face.

This alleged pheasant looks like he has just stepped out of a taxi and is readjusting his suspenders before going into the hotel. I remember Woody doing the same thing right before bursting into one of those wild laughing spells he used to suffer.

The curve in the tail could be viewed as authentic pheasant. It has that sharp downward bend of a bird suffering a narrow escape from the hay conditioner, or one who is just two wing beats faster than a load of sixes.

I prefer to believe the design on the sweater is authentic. I have too much respect for Woody Woodpecker to believe he would impersonate a Maldivian pheasant.

I probably shouldn't be critical of the sweater, but is there a husband in the world who wouldn't have said something? And is there a wife who doesn't dream of responding to these comments with heavy objects?

These things are a necessary hazard of matrimony. Whether it's knitting, needlepoint, or painting, any scene containing animals represents a sure trip to the marriage counselor.

You've seen them, too: The elk with a deer's antlers, the statuesque pointer locked-in on a covey of ducks, the magnificent white stallion with a funny little smirk on his face. They're "close, but no cigar," as they say.

The truly sensitive husband may survive the early stages of an unveiling by keeping his mouth shut, but few can pull this off smoothly. The wife will make you say something. And if that's not bad, she'll make you say something else.

The most dangerous items are those made with needlepoint or crewel. These may come in a kit, and the craftsperson can't visualize the mood of the animals until a few months of work have gone into the thing.

At this point the wily husband will not say anything negative. Being critical of a few months' work can translate into a short hospital stay.

The painters and the sculptors have a chance at least. If they are good, they can make the animals right. But the needlework people are at the mercy of pattern-makers.

I'm not being critical of artists or people who make things. I can't even paint a barn without leaving streaks. All I ask is that we watch out for the animals; They are killers.

Success

I have always been intrigued by successful people and what makes them that way. Why do some people always come out smelling like a rose, while the rest of us just come out smelling different?

Some rare combination of environment and heredity seems to give certain people the edge in whatever they do. Friends recently told my wife and me of a television program featuring interviews with TV newscaster Tom Brokaw and real estate mogul Donald Trump.

"It was really interesting," the friends said, "to listen to what these guys liked to do when they were kids. Tom Brokaw said he had a paper route when he was a kid, and anytime there was any news in the little town where he grew up, he was always the first to tell everyone. He just loved to spread the news.

"Then Donald Trump told about a train set he had as a boy, and it included buildings and bridges and things. Trump would spend days playing with that train set, building new things and rearranging the city that was part of the set."

So what did they become? Brokaw is news anchor for NBC, and Trump has built buildings and rearranged cities all over the East Coast.

"Hey, that's something, " I said. "I had a train set when I was a little kid, too. I used to haul hogs in it. I had these marbles that represented hogs, and I would tear up newspaper and put it in the pens for corn. When the hogs got fat, I'd load 'em on the train and off they went. Sometimes I hauled them in trucks, too. And I always made enough money on them to buy some more corn."

The friends just laughed. They could sense the feeling of accomplishment I felt in getting those pigs to market, and the faint note of nostalgia from one who is out of the hog business. There's nothing like seeing a big load of marbles . . . 'er hogs, leaving the place at a nice profit.

It kind of worries a person when you think about the days when we used to give the kids some toys and let them teach themselves to play. In those days, parents didn't know about the importance of educational toys and techniques for making children play creatively, like we do now.

We used to figure if it wasn't sharp and it didn't bite, it was a pretty fair toy. Now we know more about the importance of the formative years in establishing a person's personality and attitudes.

When I think of the fun I had tearing up newspapers and turning them into corn — and now I write this column that some say has nearly the same effect; The thought gives me goose acne.

It made me feel good to realize that Trump and I have so much in common: A sense of adventure, the willingness to take the big risk on a shopping center or a shipment of pigs.

Of course we do have our differences. I've been told Trump started with a nice stack of money and was able to expand his investments rather quickly.

I never have owned more than three pigs at one time and don't use the rail for shipping anymore. But I still have the same childlike confidence of my days with the electric train.

Just the other day I said to my wife, "I can't believe it, when I look at the price of hogs and the price of corn. If I had the feeding facilities and a truck to haul them in, I couldn't help but make money."

How to Count Tourists

Everyone is after the tourists these days. Rural communities are beating the drums, agencies are licking their chops, and legislatures are burping up money in an all-out effort to outsell the neighboring states — who are doing the same thing of course.

It's not entirely clear whether we are planning to create more tourists or just shuffle the ones we have around to more places.

Everybody is counting their tourists better, too. You can hardly get out of the car anymore without someone calling you a tourist.

I was just reading an Oregon columnist who says the cow business has gone navel-up again and eastern Oregon would be better off with some more national parks, so they could corral a bunch of tourists and fleece the poor devils. The general talk is that rural areas are suffering from the economic slump in agriculture and lumber sales; and we need to put our eggs in more baskets.

That's O.K. with me; but I suggest we not toss those eggs around carelessly. There are a few items in this tourism story that don't quite add up.

Now I may be wrong, as happened one other time, or I may just be jealous of all the attention the tourists are getting. However, when I read about our agricultural past and our tourism future, I become quite grumpy.

For example, it is commonly believed that a tourist and family drives into town, stops at the motel, goes to dinner, buys gas, picks up some souvenirs and a few other items, and in a day's visit the family of five has spent . . . what? Maybe $200. (This was a rich tourist.)

We can see then that each family of five tourists generates a certain amount of business. If a community can attract 50 such families per day and another 900 families with backpacks, picnic lunches, and overloaded sewage tanks on their campers, we rake in a neat sum of about $12,000 per day.

This is obviously big business,(although the figures are somewhat rough, because I just made them up).

Then what do you suppose happens when old Hank Kimball comes to town to sell his wheat? Hank has 1,000 acres of dryland crop land and produced 30 bushels per acre by the time the footrot and the stem rust got through with him; so now he sells 30,000 bushels of wheat for the worst price he ever got and takes home a cool $96,000.

But wait. Hank didn't take his money home. He couldn't afford to take it home.

He stopped to pay his fertilizer bill, and the machinery dealer, and the P.U.D., and his taxes, and the bank, and got his truck fixed, and used what was left to buy a new pair of gloves.

So you can see what Hank spent in his community was the equivalent of 8 days of hard and ruthless tourism with 950 families of five each (if you count the dog), or 7,600 Tourist Unit Days (hereafter called T.U.D.'s).

Some may retort that Hank didn't spend all of his money locally — which is true. He took three days off with the family and spent $500 on the coast for vacation, and he bought $2 worth of popcorn at an away basketball game; but that was from his wife's salary.

Now all I'm saying is that while Hank may not be flashy, he's worth a whole bunch of T.U.D.'s when it comes to supporting the rural community. And I would suggest if any legislatures have extra money lying around, it would behoove us rural folks to ask them to spend it to help old Hank Kimball get a better market for his wheat.

Fair Tour

Most folks would agree that the county fair ranks as one of the many, great cultural opportunities available in rural areas. I have always considered a good fair equivalent to four years of college and two degrees in anthropology for educational value, and slightly better than a good beating for physical conditioning.

Of course I realize that some folks have not attended a lot of fairs and may have missed a few of the more interesting aspects. Therefore, I have assumed the responsibility of taking the group on a short tour of the county fair, and will do my best to explain what's going on.

Let's begin at the front gate. This is where you get into the fair, if you can. Many fairgrounds have the front gate at the back of the grounds, or the back gate at the front, but you can almost always get in somewhere. Some folks have trouble finding the gate and like to jump over the fence, instead. The sheriff's deputies enjoy chasing these people.

Once we get into the grounds, it's just natural to head for the livestock barns, where we will be met by a group of small folks with brooms. These cheerful youngsters are on what they call "barn duty," meaning they are keeping the barn clean.

You will notice the children on barn duty are generally smaller, easier to catch, and more responsive to threats than the larger population of youth on the grounds. Be nice to the kids with the brooms; they are the good ones.

Let's mosey on over to the swine showring and watch the youngsters chase pigs with a cane (the kids have the canes). We should remember that the goal of each exhibitor in the swine show is to make his pig look good, whereas the goal of each pig is to make his exhibitor look bad.

Somewhere near the middle of the swine show you will be able to tell which exhibitors would rather be doing almost anything than making a pig look good. You will also be able to tell which pigs are having the most fun.

If we stop by the sheep show, we'll find a whole mob of sheep lined up to have their teeth checked. A person called the "judge" will walk down this line of sheep and look in each mouth to see if the teeth are nice and straight. The judge can also tell how old the sheep is by looking at its teeth.

The sheep couldn't care less, as it already knows how old it is, and has no interest in straight teeth. A sheep never smiles anyway, and only attends fairs under protest — bah!

Now let's sit down and watch the people. There's a couple of fathers talking about the crops. Their eyes are red because they have not had much sleep, or for some other reason. Don't ask.

Over there is a group of mothers, talking about the fathers. Again, don't ask.

There is the president of the county fair board. You can ask him anything; everyone else already has. The president will swear that someone else is going to have this job next year. (I wish he wouldn't swear.)

Well, it's about time to go home. We're lucky — we can go home. Some of the parents have to stay here with those kids for two more days.

Leave Your Body Be

The quest for good health has become a national epidemic. There are now millions of people who wheeze into the office each morning with scarcely the strength to lift a pencil or punch the typewriter hard enough to complete a sentence.

These people suffer from chronic exhaustion and near heart failure because they have been jogging. They believe jogging is good for them. Jogging is in fact one of the few tortures considered to be healthful. Burning at the stake may also increase blood circulation and make your feet sore, but it can't compare with jogging for weakness in the knees and pure, sincere exhaustion.

If you live in a rural area, you may have noticed that some of these healthful activities are still not widely accepted by many residents of the farming community (especially older residents). It is not uncommon for a farmer to jump in his pickup and try to help a jogger catch whatever he is chasing. Occasionally a farmer will go for the deer rifle in the hope of defending the jogger from whatever has scared him so badly.

Generally though, most folks recognize the jogger as a rural neighbor who is probably late for work or is merely running away from home again.

Joggers are not my concern, however. My concern is with the effects the crusade for health has had upon our country doctors.

It's getting to the point where you can hardly find a doctor who doesn't have some concern for your health. I don't mean concern for what's wrong with you. I'm talking about concern for your health.

Many readers will remember the old-fashioned country doctor who would treat you for what ails you and leave the rest alone. A man could go into the Doc's office and say, "I've got this terrible wheezing sound in my chest. What do you suppose is causing it?"

Doc would say, "It's your lungs." He wouldn't make personal comments about how many cigars you smoke each day or suggest you donate your leftover organs to science. Or say, "Can I have your shotgun?" No, sir! He would just tell you what was wrong with you.

Nowadays, doctors are into maintenance and prevention. They want you to be healthy, fulltime.

Of course, the old-time doctors were operating in the era before transplanting organs became popular. In those days there really wasn't much point in saving your liver, after you had already ruined your lungs.

We used to think a person should consume more alcohol after the age of 40 in order to prevent thickening of the blood. Theory had it that if you ate more fats and fried foods, drank more wine, and smoked a cigar after each meal, the heart, liver, and lungs should go out at about the same time. There wasn't much left over in those days.

Now everyone is becoming so healthy that quite a business has sprung up in organ transplanting. I'll tell you one thing though, if you ever need a new set of knees, you won't get them from those guys out there jogging up and down the road.

Other Books by Roger Pond

THINGS THAT GO "BAA!" IN THE NIGHT
TALES FROM A COUNTRY KID
(Humor)

MY DOG WAS A REDNECK BUT WE GOT HIM FIXED
TALES FROM THE BACK FORTY
(Humor)

THE LIVESTOCK SHOWMAN'S HANDBOOK:
A GUIDE TO RAISING ANIMALS FOR JUNIOR LIVESTOCK SHOWS
(Informational)

Order Form

Pine Forest Publishing
314 Pine Forest Road
Goldendale, WA 98620
Phone: 509-773-4718

Quantity	Item	Price	Total
	It's Hard To Look Cool When Your Car's Full Of Sheep (Humor)	$11.95	
	Things that go "Baa!" in the Night (Humor)	$11.95	
	My Dog Was A Redneck, But We Got Him Fixed (Humor)	$11.95	
	Livestock Showman's Handbook (Informational)	$17.95	
	Book Total		
	Postage & Handling: $2.00 per book		
	Washington residents: Please add 7% sales tax		
	Grand Total		

Payment must accompany order.
Make checks payable to *Pine Forest Publishing*.

Name _____

Address _____

City _____ State _____ Zip _____

Phone _____